SERGEI II

Her Russian Protector, Book 5.5

Roxie Rivera

Night Works Books
College Station, Texas

Night Works Books
3515-B Longmire Drive #103
College Station, Texas 77845
www.roxierivera.com

Publisher's Note: This is a work of fiction. Names, characters, places, and incidents are a product of the author's imagination. Locales and public names are sometimes used for atmospheric purposes. Any resemblance to actual people, living or dead, or to businesses, companies, events, institutions, or locales is completely coincidental.

Book Layout ©2013 BookDesignTemplates.com

Ordering Information:
Quantity sales. Special discounts are available on quantity purchases by corporations, associations, and others. For details, contact the "Special Sales Department" at the address above.

SERGEI II (Her Russian Protector #5.5)/ Roxie Rivera. -- 1st ed.
ISBN 978-1-63042-021-5

Acknowledgements

First, a very huge thanks to Rimma for answering all of my silly (and not so silly!) questions about Russian language and culture. Any mistakes in the book are mine and mine alone.

Second, a high-five to Jayha for making me laugh with her colorful tales of family reunions and ratchet potato salad.

1 CHAPTER ONE

Stretching my arms overhead, I inhaled a deep, slow breath and gradually awakened to the sound of a running shower. Blinking, I rolled onto my side and slid my hand over the empty space next to me. The sheets were still warm under my palm. Unable to help myself, I lowered my face to the silky cotton and pressed my nose against the fabric to inhale that familiar, comforting scent of eucalyptus and *him* that made every morning utter perfection.

Sergei.

My Sergei.

Smiling like the Cheshire cat, I dragged his pillow closer and tugged the sheet that was twisted around my thick hips up around my naked breasts. Hugging his pillow, I let the memories of yet another torrid night together warm me. Since discovering I was pregnant, Sergei had been insatiable yet so tender with me. For such a powerful giant, he could be incredibly gentle when the moment called for it. It amazed me sometimes that those big hands that had so brutally pummeled his opponents glided over my curves with the lightest touch of a feather.

But even though his touch was soft and his pace languid, Sergei still managed to make me see stars at least twice a night. *Four last night*, I thought with a naughty giggle and burrowed against his pillow. I didn't remember much after the third climax he had coaxed from me with that wickedly skilled mouth of his, but what I did remember left my body thrumming with a sensual heat.

"You're awake."

My eyelids parted as his gruff, rumbling voice made my belly flutter. I found him leaning against the frame of the open bathroom door. With a towel wrapped around his waist, he eyed me in that predatory way of his. I let my appreciative gaze travel across those wide shoulders and his insanely sculpted chest. The bruises from the tournament had finally faded to a pale yellow, the edges rimmed with darker spots of purple and even green. My gaze moved over his abs right down to the dark trail that stretched from his navel to the top of the towel. Knowing what he had hidden beneath that towel made everything feminine in me sing with joy.

Mine. Mine. Mine. He's all mine.

"I'll be quieter tomorrow." He pushed off the door frame. "I wanted to let you sleep in this morning."

"You didn't wake me."

Sergei snatched up a piece of ginger candy from the box on the bedside table and unwrapped it. He eased onto the bed beside me and held it up to my lips. I accepted the little treat that seemed to be keeping my morning sickness under control. The evening of the barbecue we had hosted for friends, I had been hit with the first really awful wave of it. After our guests had left and I had curled up in bed, he had disappeared to the store and had returned with just about everything ginger the twenty-four-hour drugstore had on its shelves.

While I let the small candy dissolve on my tongue, he ran his hand along my thigh. The heat of his palm blazed a trail through the sheet. His hand slid higher and finally rested on my belly. "You need more rest." He rubbed a slow circle there. "You're doing hard work growing my baby."

The reverent way he spoke the words made my heart swell with love. Getting pregnant so unexpectedly hadn't been part of the plan, but I didn't regret that one night we had made love without protection, not for a single moment. Becoming a mother was a daunting prospect, but I could facing anything with Sergei beside me.

He traced a heart on my stomach, and I smiled at the sweet gesture. "What do you think it is, Bianca?"

"I don't know." I bit my lip. "Do you have a feeling?"

"No."

"Do you have a preference?"

He continued to draw shapes. "A healthy baby is all I want." His mouth twitched with the hint of a grin. "If it's a girl, I'm going to be gray before she's even out of high school. She'll probably have a thing for bad boys like her mama."

I laughed and covered his hand with mine. "I don't have a thing for bad boys. I have a thing for one very bad boy in particular."

He leaned forward and cupped the back of my neck. Teasing his lips against mine, he claimed my mouth in a lingering kiss. His thumb brushed my cheek, and he pulled back to gaze into my eyes. "You're so beautiful in the morning. This is my favorite way to see you."

I lifted a skeptical eyebrow. "Oh, really? With my hair a mess and my face blotchy and—"

"You look like you were thoroughly fucked last night," he said in that blunt way of his. "You look like a woman who came so hard that she passed out with a smile on her face." His sexy grin made my heart race. "Seeing you this way makes me proud of my work. You're always so perfectly put together. I like knowing I'm the only one who can make you look like this."

"Well," I said quietly, "when you put it like that..."

"Bianca?" He tipped my chin with his fingers until our gazes met. "I love you."

My heart soared. "I love you, too."

I didn't think I would ever get tired of hearing him say those three words. I had never expected that I would win the heart of a man like Sergei. Sometimes I still couldn't quite believe that he had chosen me. With his outrageously good looks and that killer body, he could have had any woman—and had done just that. But for some reason, it was me that he had fallen for after one meeting. It was me that he had chased for five months. He had kicked down a door for me and so much more.

He had left the mob for me, for *us*, and I would never, ever forget that. We had beaten the odds to be together, and I would fight until my dying breath to protect the life we were building. The searing heat of the love reflected in his eyes told me he would do the same thing. Without question or hesitation, he would fight for us.

"I'm going to pick up a new suitcase while I'm out today. Do you need anything?"

I shook my head. "I'm good on the luggage front."

"Are you sure you still want to go to London?" His gaze fell to my stomach. "If you're too tired or don't feel well, I'm sure Vivian wouldn't mind."

"I know she wouldn't, but I would. I feel fine. Really," I added, certain he was worrying too much. "Pregnant women travel all the time. Besides, this is Vivi's first international art show. I want to be there."

"So do I, but I would feel better about you going if you were able to see your doctor first."

"They can't fit me in until we get back from London. I spoke to the nurse-midwife for, like, twenty minutes on the phone. She said that as long as I'm not cramping or spotting, there's nothing to worry about and that they prefer to see patients around eight weeks. I'm not even six weeks, Sergei. Lots of my friends didn't get in for their first prenatal visits until ten or eleven weeks."

"I don't like it," he grumbled.

"You worry too much." I sat up a little higher against the pillows and didn't even bother to tug the sheet up to cover my chest. Just as expected, Sergei's hand immediately covered my bare breast. He seemed to remember how sensitive I was as he cradled my flesh so carefully.

"I love you, and you're pregnant with my baby. I'm supposed to worry." His thumb drew a lazy circle around my nipple. With a note of awe in his voice, he murmured, "You're starting to change. See?"

I noticed how much darker my skin looked, the puckered peaks the deepest shade of cocoa and so much different than his lighter, tanned skin. "From what I've heard, this is the first of many changes."

His finger trailed along the swell of my breast and up toward my collarbone. "Are we doing anything tonight?"

"I have that meeting with Mama."

Sergei's lips settled into a grim line. "Oh. *That.*"

"Yes. *That.*" Once a month, I attended a support group for families who had lost a loved one to murder. My mother had been the local chapter's president until the stroke and ensuing complications that had taken her leg and left her hospitalized for months. Even while in recovery, she had never stopped working as a victim and family advocate. Now she was getting back into the swing of things, and I was happy to share the load with her. "You could come with us. It might be good for you to talk about—"

"No." He cut me off quickly, but I wasn't easily shut down.

"You could talk about your brother and his wife and your nieces," I finished my thought.

"And say what?" He stared at me with an expression of incredulity. "My name is Sergei, and my brother and his family were slaughtered by a mob crew in Moscow because he had been laundering money for terrorists?"

He had a point. "You could say they were killed by criminals—"

"And then what? I tell them that I got my justice by selling myself to a different mob outfit who killed every single last one of those men who took my family?" He shook his head. "That's a chapter of my life we've closed, Bianca. It's done. It's finished. There's nothing to be gained from talking about my brother or his family."

"What about peace, Sergei?"

"Peace?" He laughed harshly. "Bianca, there's no peace to be had on that score. I've accepted that they're gone. All the talking in the world isn't going to bring them back."

"It's not about bringing them back," I hotly retorted. "It's about honoring their memories. It's about finding a way to forgive the people who hurt you. It's about finding a way to live every day with that gaping, raw wound that losing someone to murder leaves behind."

"Forgive?" He practically spat the word. "Forgiveness is weakness."

With all the hormones raging through my body, my emotions were too close to the surface. My eyes prickled with heat, and I felt the first tears drip onto my cheeks. Annoyed with myself for getting so worked up, I snapped at Sergei. "Why do you have to belittle this?"

He looked utterly crushed and ashamed. Cupping my face, he whispered my name and wiped away the tears. "Bianca, *milaya moya*, I didn't mean to upset you. I'm sorry. It was stupid of me. I didn't mean to belittle your work. I know what this group means to you." He kissed my forehead. "I'm sorry. You're a better woman than me to find forgiveness for your brother's killer. I can't. I just—I can't."

Knowing the life he had escaped, where a weakness could get him killed, I accepted that forgiveness was beyond the scope of possibility for him. Feeling even worse for blowing our disagreement out of proportion, I inhaled a ragged breath. "I'm sorry. I didn't mean to flip out like this."

"It's all right." He rubbed my back and pressed his lips to mine. "You're pregnant. I think this is normal." He nuzzled our noses together before capturing my mouth in a loving kiss. "I understand that it brings you peace to talk about your brother and to fight for other victims. I admire that about you and your mother. I truly do—but it's not for me."

I gripped his hand. "I understand."

"We're okay?"

I nodded. "We're okay."

"Good." He lifted my hand and kissed my fingers. "Would you like to bring your mother over for dinner? I can cook."

"Is this your way of reminding me that we haven't told her about the baby yet?"

"This is my way of suggesting we do it sooner rather than later," he replied honestly. "She needs to find out before we tell my family when they meet us in London next week."

"I know."

Sergei tapped the tip of my nose. "Why are you so afraid to tell her? She's your mother, and she loves you."

"I know that."

"But?"

"But she's old-fashioned when it comes to things like this," I murmured. Until Sergei, I had been an old-fashioned kind of girl myself. The thought of having a baby before marriage had always secretly scandalized me. How many brides had come through the front door of my family's wedding boutique with tiny baby bumps? I had artfully concealed those round tummies with pleats and tulle and empire waists all the while silently judging those women for being careless. Now who was the careless one?

"She'll love this baby as much as she loves you," he reassured me. "She might not be happy about the circumstances, but she'll come around, Bianca."

"It's not just that," I admitted finally. "I feel guilty for taking away the white wedding dreams she's probably always had for me. We're in the business of happy endings and beautiful fairy-tale weddings. I'm sure she dreamed of the way it would be for me, her only daughter, and now she'll have to be happy with a shotgun wedding."

As soon as the words were out of my mouth, I wanted to die. We hadn't even discussed marriage yet, but that hadn't stopped me from blurting out the words like a fool. I nervously glanced at Sergei who appeared totally unruffled by the statement hanging in the air.

Leaning forward, he kissed me so sweetly. With a smile that made my heart do wild flips in my chest, he promised, "It won't be a shotgun wedding. I'll make it beautiful for you. Perfect," he added and kissed me again. "It will be everything you deserve."

His promise made, Sergei slid off the bed and grabbed some clothing from the dresser we now shared. His calm, assured reply left me so curious. As he tugged on his workout clothes, I managed not to pester him with the million questions racing through my head. I trusted that when he was ready, he would ask.

"I'll be at the warehouse with Ivan until ten and then I'm heading over to the construction offices." He tugged on his sneakers and sat on the edge of the bed to tie them. "Do you want me to make your breakfast before I leave?"

I shook my head. "I might sneak in a few more minutes of sleep before I get up for work."

He rubbed my earlobe between his fingers. "Take it easy today. Stay off your feet and drink plenty of water. It's going to be hot today so wear something light."

Smiling at the way he was so overprotective, I simply nodded. "I will."

Sergei sneaked one final kiss. "I love you. Call me if you need anything."

"I love you, too." I watched him cross the bedroom and silently counted his steps. Just as he always did, he paused in the doorway and stared at me for a moment. It was as if he wanted to memorize exactly what I looked like. I sensed that it was the way he reassured himself this was real. He had won me and my love. We were now forever entwined.

Our lives had changed so drastically in the last week. I wasn't surprised he needed to remind himself that this was actually happening. No longer an enforcer and prize fighter for mob boss Nikolai Kalasnikov, Sergei was his own man now. He was going to be a father...and a husband.

My husband, I thought, with an excited thrill. Our relationship had broken all of my rules, and it wasn't the perfect storybook romance, but I didn't care.

It was *ours*. And that was all that mattered.

Arms crossed, Sergei stood outside one of the sparring rings in Ivan Markovic's world-class training center and watched the pair of fighters striking each other. Since leaving Nikolai's service, he had been tasked with finding a replacement prize fighter for the boss. Watching these two kids halfheartedly trading punches, he sighed heavily. No, these boys wouldn't do either. They were both afraid to get hit and feared pain. Fear had no place in the ring. It was the easiest way for a man to get hurt.

Growling like a damned bear, Ivan shouted an instruction at the dark-haired fighter and then leaped the ropes with the ease and grace of a smaller, lither man. The sleeveless shirt he wore displayed his thick, tattooed arms. Here in the comfort of his gym, Ivan didn't bother to cover up the marks that told the world about the violent, sinful life he had once lived.

Sergei watched the two kids in the ring staring openly at the tattoos. He had been the same way once, filled with awe and fear as he looked upon Ivan for the first time.

Sergei smirked as his mentor ripped into the young street soldiers who had been plucked from Nikolai's ranks to try their hands at bare-knuckle fighting. By the looks on their faces, they wanted to get back to making collections. He didn't blame them. Ivan was the only man in the world that Sergei couldn't take in a fight, and that was saying something.

Cursing in every language he knew, Ivan slipped between the ropes and joined Sergei as the two kids started fighting again. "Can you believe this shit? How the hell do these boys survive out there?"

Sergei shrugged and kept an eye on the two younger men who were trying to follow Ivan's instructions as they continued to spar. "It's a different game than when you were on the streets. Hell, it's a different game than when *I* started."

"Soft," Ivan snarled. "They're weak."

Hearing the way Ivan practically spat the word *weak*, Sergei remembered the way he had upset Bianca that morning. He rubbed the back of his neck as shame engulfed him. He hadn't meant it to come out so harshly. He hated the way he became so defensive when it came to that mess back in Moscow. Now that Bianca had freed him from that life, he wanted to put as much distance between himself and those old ugly memories as possible. Going to a support group meeting to sit around and rip open that scabbed over wound? It wasn't fucking happening.

"You okay?" Ivan shot him a strange look.

He waved his hand. "I said something stupid this morning. It made Bianca cry."

Ivan winced and reached forward to grab the taut rope in front of him. "Seems to be a lot of that stupidity going around this week."

He eyed his mentor and friend. "You and Erin?"

Ivan nodded stiffly. "The honeymoon is over. It was only a matter of time until we had our first real argument."

He wanted to ask what the newlyweds had fought over, but he didn't. It wasn't any of his business, yet he couldn't help but wonder about his own relationship with Bianca. Ivan and Erin had been together for a year, and they absolutely adored each other. Their love was unshakable and strong. He didn't know whether he should find the revelation that they fought a comfort or a concern, considering the relatively short length of his relationship with Bianca.

"Ten is getting out of prison tomorrow. I offered him one of the rooms in our house until he gets back on his feet. Erin didn't take that news very well."

Sergei had never met the ruthless enforcer everyone called Ten, but if the chilling stories told by the crews were even half true, he didn't want Anton Vasiliev anywhere near Bianca. Surprised by Ivan's admission, he said, "No, I can't imagine she would."

"It's not about his record or even what he did for the family that made her mad," Ivan explained. "It's about her sister. I won't let Ruby live with us if she ever gets out of prison."

"Because?"

"Because she's a fucking junkie who nearly got Erin killed," Ivan growled matter-of-factly. "Ruby knows how to twist Erin around her finger and manipulate her. I won't let Ruby hurt Erin again. That's a pain that cuts too deep." He exhaled a rough breath. "Erin trusts that I know Ten well enough to judge his character. He's safe to have in the house. He's done extremely violent things, but he's not a violent man."

Sergei chortled. "Is there a difference?"

Ivan pinned him in place with an icy gaze. "You tell me. Should I list all the things you did for Nikolai?"

Duly chastised, Sergei clenched his teeth and nodded. "Yeah. Okay."

"Ten did his job, and he did it well. When that robbery got fucked up, he stepped forward and took the heat to protect the family. He went inside for six years. Six. Years." Ivan emphasized with a jab of his meaty, scarred finger. "We owe him a new start."

"In your house?" Sergei shook his head. "Put him in an apartment or send him to live with someone else."

"He's my friend." Ivan watched the fighters in the ring, but Sergei could tell he wasn't paying any attention to them. He was thinking of Ten and of the history they shared. "He needs people he trusts around him now."

"And Erin? What does she need?"

Ivan shot him a warning look. "My wife is my business. When you have a wife, you'll understand that."

"Give me a few weeks, and I'll understand." He grumbled the words under his breath, but Ivan's keen hearing picked them out even over the din of raucous music blaring over the speakers and the noise of the gym.

His mentor narrowed his eyes at him and then called out to the fighters in the ring. "You two are done. Cool down. Get showered. Get the hell out of my warehouse."

The younger of the two fighters tugged his mouthpiece free while the other one bailed as quickly as possible and practically ran for the locker room. Panting and slicked with sweat, the blond asked, "What time do I come back tomorrow?"

Ivan laughed harshly. "You want more of this punishment?"

The kid shrugged. "It's the only way I'll learn."

Sergei didn't let it show that he was impressed by the kid's hunger to prove himself. He was lean and scrappy, but there was room for improvement as long as he had heart. "What's your name?"

"Boy."

"Boy?"

"Boychenko," the kid answered. The only accent to his voice was a slight hint of that Texas drawl that colored his vowel sounds in the same way it did Bianca's. "Roman Boychenko."

"You're with Arty?" Sergei held up three fingers to differentiate the Artyom he meant from the other one that ran in their circle. Boy nodded, and Sergei glanced at Ivan. If the kid was trusted to run collections for Arty, that was a good enough recommendation for Sergei. A clipped bob of Ivan's head confirmed his thoughts. "Be here at six tomorrow morning. Go easy on your breakfast or else you'll be mopping up his floors."

"Yes, sir."

Sergei watched the kid climb out of the ring and start a cool down circuit. Turning to Ivan, he made a face. "Sir?"

Ivan clapped him on the back. "You're getting old."

"Old? I'm not even thirty-five!"

"When you were nineteen, how old did thirty seem?"

Sergei grunted, and Ivan laughed. Hooking a thumb toward his office, he said, "Let's talk."

When they were safely inside Ivan's office, he leaned against the door and waited. With his huge, inked arms crossed in front of his chest, Ivan looked every bit the undefeated underground champion he had been when he had retired from Nikolai's service and Sergei had taken his place. Now he trained elite fighters who fought for huge purses in tournaments and on cable television. He was one of the most sought after coaches in the mixed-martial arts world and hugely successful—and Sergei wanted to be just like him.

"Have you thought about my offer?"

"I have."

"And?"

Sergei sighed. "I want to take your job offer, but if I go full-time with you, I have to give up the construction piece the boss gave me. I can't do both."

"You don't have to do both. You work for me and take your cut from the construction." He said it so easily. "The boss doesn't expect you to swing a hammer eighty hours a week. He gave you that action as a reward for all you did for him and for the family."

"It doesn't feel right to take the money without doing the work."

"Do you have any idea how much money he made off your fists?"

Considering his own small winnings, Sergei had a good idea of the prize money Nikolai had won off his fights. "I need to square it with him first. I need to keep that construction income. Bringing my family over won't be cheap, and then there's Bianca."

Ivan studied him for an unnerving moment. "Is she making you pay her back for buying you from the boss?"

He shook his head. "No. She calls it a gift. A gift," he repeated with a rough laugh. "Can you believe that?"

"Yes, I believe it. She loves you. She fought for you. There's no sweeter woman in the world than one who will fight for you."

Certain that he could trust Ivan and desperate to tell someone, he confessed, "Bianca is pregnant."

Ivan's arms dropped to his sides in shock. "Pregnant?"

Sergei nodded. "It was only one night, one time, but..."

"That's all it takes." Ivan reached back and gripped the desk behind him. "Is she upset?"

"No, she was surprised. We both were, but now she's happy. We're both excited."

"That's good. It's easier that way." Ivan hesitated. "Are you going to marry her?"

"Of course!" He couldn't believe Ivan even had to ask.

"Because you love her or—"

"Because I love her," Sergei interjected. "Because I want a family with her."

A broad smile brightened Ivan's hard face. "I'm happy for you. It's good to have a woman like Bianca in your life. She's strong. She'll make you a better man."

Sergei understood that Ivan was thinking of the way Erin had changed and softened him. "I'm luckier than I deserve."

Ivan waved his hand as if to argue that point. "When are you going to ask her?"

"Soon," he said. "I've already made some plans."

"Do you have a ring?"

When he shook his head, Ivan pushed off his desk and strolled around to the back side of it. He opened a drawer, retrieved his wallet and plucked a business card from inside it. "Here. Go see Kazimir. He's the best in town. We've all used him. He did beautiful work for Erin. You've seen Vivian's rings?"

"Yes." They were so perfectly her. The boss had chosen well.

"Kazimir keeps settings that only need center stones on hand. You'll find something for Bianca there."

Sergei accepted the card. "Thank you."

"When you walk in the door, he'll take one look at you and recognize you as Nikolai's enforcer, but just in case he doesn't, you tell him I sent you. He'll take care of you."

And there it was. The way their world worked. No doubt this jeweler gave discounts to Nikolai's friends in exchange for some sort of perk—protection, a cheaper source of materials, side deals that helped him beat his competitors. Nothing came free in this world. Nothing.

"Listen," Ivan said carefully, his tone strained, "have you talked to your family about Bianca yet?"

"They know they'll be meeting Bianca in London. They know she saved me."

Ivan drummed his thick fingers on his desk. "Have you told them *everything* about her?"

A long, uncomfortable moment of silence stretched between them. Finally, Sergei said, "They know she's not like us."

Not like us. Not Russian or white. He didn't have to say the words Ivan was undoubtedly thinking. They were thoughts that had been troubling him since finding out Bianca was pregnant. He refused to burden her with the what-ifs while she was in such a delicate state, but it was possible that Lidia might have been right about his mother. She wouldn't dislike Bianca simply because of the color of her skin, but those old ingrained ideas about what was right and what was not weren't going to be easy to change. He hoped that the idea of a grandchild would soften his mother's feelings, but if it didn't...

"These things..." Ivan's voice trailed off as he seemed to be searching for the right words. "Look, we live *here* now. It's different here. Your family will meet Bianca and see how sweet she is. They'll understand how far she went to save you. They'll forget about everything else."

And if they don't? It was the question that wouldn't stop tormenting him.

Ivan stepped closer and squeezed his shoulder. "It will all work out in the end. Yes?"

With a smile that didn't reach his eyes, Sergei nodded and left the office after a quick discussion about Boy's training. After showering and changing into jeans and a polo shirt, he headed for the exit. He glanced toward Ivan's office and was surprised to see Erin walking toward her husband. As usual, she wore a flirty little dress that made her seem so carefree and innocent.

Slowing his steps, he watched the pair interact. The regret darkening Ivan's eyes and tightening his expression was clear enough. He held out one big hand, his knuckles gnarled and tattooed so heavily, and Erin smiled so sweetly at him. She interlaced their fingers and tugged him toward his office. Like a puppy trailing its master, Ivan followed her into the office and promptly shut the door. A moment later, Ivan stepped in front of the window and started to close the blinds.

Smirking and laughing softly to himself, Sergei decided that Ruby wasn't the only one who could wrap someone around her finger. Erin had managed to do what no other person had—she had tamed the beast and had him eating right out of the palm of her pretty little hand. He had no doubts that the couple would work out their disagreement.

Sergei sat in his SUV until the air conditioner cooled the interior. He smacked the card Ivan had given him against the steering wheel and decided to go see the jeweler first. Once he had the ring sorted, he would make one more stop before hitting the construction offices.

After listening to Bianca voice her fears about her mother's reaction to the news, he wanted to spare her any ugliness. If anyone was going to bear the brunt of Mrs. Bradshaw's anger, it should be him. He was the one who had seduced Bianca that night and persuaded her to let him make love to her without any barriers between their bodies. If her mother wanted to hand out a scolding, he would take it right on the chin and spare Bianca the worst. He had sworn to protect Bianca, and he meant to do that.

As he backed out of his parking space, Sergei felt an unfamiliar quiver of panic hit his gut. He had a sneaking suspicion Bianca's mother was going to make him work for her blessing and permission to marry her daughter.

With a snort of laughter, he decided that the same trick that had endeared him to Bianca wasn't likely to work on her mother. Kicking down her front door to save her from a shower curtain? Not a chance in hell of that one winning over Mrs. Bradshaw.

He would think of something. He always did. Once he had Bianca's mother squared away, he would concentrate on an even bigger problem—his own mother

2 CHAPTER TWO

When Sergei entered the jewelry store, he immediately noticed Nikolai Kalasnikov standing at the glass counter on the far left side. His gaze skipped around the room, counting up the four other customers, and landed on Kostya who lingered just off to the right side of the door, ever vigilant and ready to protect the boss. Just a few short days ago, that had been Sergei's job. He felt suddenly strange to be in the same space as his old boss but totally apart from that world.

Glancing back toward the sound of the opening and closing door, Nikolai did a double take. A true smile curved his mouth. "Sergei."

"Boss." He might not be on Nikolai's payroll any-more, but the man was *the* boss of Houston.

"Shopping for Bianca?" Nikolai leaned an elbow on the glass case and eyed him with amusement. "Surely you aren't in need of an apology present so soon?"

"No." Sergei laughed and joined the boss at the counter. He was surprised when the other man held out his hand. Grasping it firmly, he shook it. "I'm here to look at those."

Nikolai followed his pointing finger to the case of engagement rings. His eyes widened slightly. "I see."

Not wanting to discuss the reason behind their rushed engagement, Sergei said, "Ivan sent me here. He said this is the best place."

The boss seemed to understand that he wasn't go-ing to share any more than he had already revealed so he didn't push. "It is. Every piece I've ever given Vee has come from here. Kaz has good taste." He uncov-ered the jewelry sitting on white cloth. "See?"

A brilliant gold and diamond necklace glittered un-der the bright lights. The design made Sergei smile. Nikolai had commissioned a beautiful sunburst pen-dant for Vivian. Matching sunburst earrings and a del-icate bracelet completed the set. The thoughtfulness behind the gift showed how much the boss adored and cherished his young wife. He called her his sun because she was the bright light that illuminated his darkness.

"I wanted to get her something special for the art show next week." Nikolai brushed his fingers over the diamonds. "She deserves it."

"Yes." He had been her bodyguard long enough to know how very hard she worked. How many evenings had he simply sat in a corner and stared at the pieces lining the walls of her studio while she splashed paint on canvas and swirled her brushes around a palette? Like Bianca, he hoped Vivian's upcoming show opened more doors for her career. Her paintings were beautiful and haunting. He wanted so many more people to see her talent.

Covering up the jewelry, Nikolai turned his attention to the nearby engagement ring case. "What do you think Bianca will like?"

Sergei shadowed Nikolai to the case and studied the display. "It has to be delicate. Not too big or flashy," he added. "She works with her hands all day. I want her to be able to wear the ring without it snagging on the dresses at her shop."

Nikolai made a humming sound in agreement. "Princess cut? Asscher? Cushion?"

Sergei blinked. He had no idea what the hell the boss meant. "Uh...square?"

Nikolai laughed and tapped the glass. "You want a princess cut."

Certain he would be making many trips to this store in the future, Sergei made a mental note to do some jewelry research. As he scanned the rings in the case, his gaze flickered over one in particular and swung back to reconsider it. There were two rows of winking diamonds in a rounded square shape surrounding an open slot meant for a larger center stone. The shoulder and mounting had detailed open scrollwork done in platinum with more diamonds.

"That's very nice," Nikolai murmured his approval. "I think it's a setting meant for a round stone though."

"Round, square," Sergei said with a shrug. "It's pretty." *Like her.*

Finished helping his customer, the shop's owner sauntered over and held out his hand. Nikolai made introductions. After shaking hands, the older man produced a key to unlock the case. "Have you found something you like?"

Sergei indicated the ring. "Can I see this one?"

"Of course." Kazimir reached in and removed the tray holding the ring Sergei had been admiring. Holding it up for Sergei's inspection, he said, "A beautiful ring for a beautiful woman."

Smiling, Sergei took the ring and inspected it carefully. The craftsmanship was superb. He imagined the diamonds and platinum adorning Bianca's finger.

There was no need to look at other rings. This was the one.

"If you like this one, my daughter has the sketch for a matching wedding band." Kazimir motioned toward the back of the shop. "Would you like to look at some center stones?"

"Yes." Sergei handed the ring back to the owner.

"This setting is for a round diamond. A carat or thereabouts," he added. "Let me go in the back and bring out a selection for you."

While they waited for the jeweler to return with the diamonds, Nikolai made small talk. "Did you see Vanya this morning?"

Sergei nodded. "We tossed one of the kids you sent."

"Which one did you keep?"

"Boychenko."

Nikolai seemed surprised by that. "He's small."

"Everyone is smaller than me," he said easily. "He's not as big as some of the other fighters on the circuit, but he's fast. He can learn."

"He won't ever be you," Nikolai groused. "There will never be another you. After Vanya left, I was lucky to have you fall into my hands. Now?" He shook his head. "I don't foresee many wins in our future."

Sergei noted the way the boss said *our*. Even though he was out of the family, he was still considered part of it. He wondered if he would ever truly be out of that life. Even Ivan and Alexei Sarnov couldn't completely cut their ties. Ivan continued to train fighters for the boss, and Alexei provided trucks from his fleet whenever the boss needed them.

"Look, boss, when you have time, I'd like to talk about the construction company." Nikolai's eyes narrowed fractionally. It was a twitch Sergei had learned to see as a warning so he decided to tread very carefully. "Ivan offered me a job at his warehouse."

The lines eased around the boss's mouth. "The gym is a better fit for you now, but there's a better future in the construction. For you and your family," he gestured to the engagement rings with a lift of his chin. "David wants to retire in the next two or three years so you'll stay with the company and take over when he leaves. You'll learn from him and then you'll have something legitimate that's yours."

"Mine?" Sergei couldn't hide his shock. He had never been anything more than a soldier in the organization. To be given something this big? It wasn't the usual way of things.

"Yours." Nikolai spun his wedding band around his finger. "I trust you. It's that simple for me. It takes a lot for a man to earn my trust."

Sergei held the boss's steely gaze. The message was broadcast loud and clear. *So don't fuck this up or I'll fuck you up.* Hoping Nikolai understood how much this meant to him, he said, "Thank you, boss."

"You've earned it. I asked much of you when you were mine. You risked your life in that cage night after night and never complained. A good living for your family is the least I can do."

Sergei swallowed hard. Before he could find a way to show his gratitude, Nikolai asked, "Did you hear about Ten?"

"Yes." He didn't mention the part about Ten moving in with Ivan and Erin.

"I've decided that he's going to take your place. He's going to be Vee's new guard."

Considering the brutal way Ten had attended to the shadowy side of the family's business, Sergei figured Vee couldn't have been in more capable hands. Thinking of the many months he had spent as her guard and the years he had known her before that, Sergei respectfully warned, "She won't like him."

"I'm not paying him to be her friend. I'm paying him to keep her safe." Then, with a slanted dip of his head, Nikolai asked, "Would you speak with him? You understand her. You know what she likes and what she needs from her guards. It will be easier for her if Ten understands her...quirks."

Sergei chuckled softly. "Quirks? Sure, boss, I'll tell him all about her quirks."

With a hint of amusement playing on his face, Ni-kolai said, "Perhaps not all of them. I don't want Ten asking for a job as a dishwasher or a busboy at Samovar instead."

Thinking of how difficult Vivian could sometimes be, Sergei could only laugh.

"They don't have to be best friends like you two were, but I want him to treat her with the same kindness that you always showed her. Especially now," Nikolai added softly.

As far as Sergei knew, the couple still hadn't breathed a word about Vivian's pregnancy. The rumblings on the street about problems brewing between her father and the cartel he once served had everyone on edge. There were whispers that Maksim Prokhorov, the big boss out of Moscow, had made a deal with Romero Valero to run guns and more in Guzman cartel territory. Not surprisingly the move was making everyone nervous. If the cartel wanted to hit back, they would start with Vivian—and then there really would be hell to pay.

Kazimir returned with a blonde in tow. Sergei noticed the resemblance between the pair and figured this was the daughter. While her father wore a tailored three piece suit complete with pocket watch, she had chosen a slim-fitting black pencil skirt and emerald green top that made her pale blonde hair seem as white as snow. She had intensely blue eyes, the color as deep as the sapphires on sale in her father's store. He glanced at the nametag pinned to her shirt. *Zoya.*

Although she spoke to Nikolai in perfect Russian, there was no mistaking that accent. Like Boy, she was American-born. Judging by the proud way her father smiled at her, she was the center of his world. When she studied the ring Sergei had chosen, she grinned approvingly. "Oh, Bianca will definitely love this."

Stunned to hear Zoya talk with such authority on Bianca, he asked, "You know Bianca?"

"She runs a wedding boutique, and I'm in the business of diamonds. We're at most of the same wedding expos and attend get-togethers for wedding professionals." She slipped the ring onto her pointer finger. "I had heard through friends that you two were dating. Congratulations."

She seemed genuinely happy for them, so he accepted with a smile. "Thank you."

Nikolai clapped him on the back. "I have a meeting or else I'd stay to help you pick out the perfect stone." He glanced at Kazimir and Zoya. "They'll take care of you."

"Yes, of course," the jeweler hurriedly assured. "Everything will be perfect."

"Good." Nikolai gave instructions for the gifts he had commissioned for his wife and bid them all farewell. Sergei turned to wave at Kostya before giving his attention to the line of bright, shiny diamonds waiting for him on a black velvet tray.

One by one, Zoya and her father went through the handful of stones they had selected. They explained how the diamonds were graded by color and cut and let him inspect them until he found one that he liked best. "I need this ring before we leave for London next week."

"It's not a problem," Kazimir promised. "We've done much faster turnarounds than that."

"We'll need her ring size," Zoya said as she tucked the diamond and the setting into a small envelope she had labeled with all of his details.

Prepared for that, Sergei tugged his wallet from his jeans and retrieved the loop of dental floss he had wrapped around Bianca's finger while she slept that morning. "Will this work?"

Zoya giggled when she took it from him. "Yes. This is actually perfect." Dropping the floss measurement into the envelope, she asked, "Would you like me to start on a sketch for the wedding bands? I've got one that matches this, but I think Bianca would like something a little thinner. Maybe with an inlay?"

"I'd like to see some drawings when we get back from London."

"I'll be sure to have some ready for you." She jotted some notes on an order form and turned it around for him to examine. The tip of her pen moved down the bulleted points of the store's policies and then she touched the estimated final price for the ring. Her pen slid a little lower to the discount they were giving him. It seemed almost too generous, but he wasn't about to argue. "Does this work for you?"

"Yes." He took the pen and scrawled his name in the right spot. Zoya shook his hand, congratulated him again and then wished him a safe trip to London. As he left the jewelry store, he started thinking about what he would say when the time came to propose. He had a vague idea of the words he would use. It needed to be heartfelt but maybe humorous, too. She would appreciate that.

Back in his SUV, Sergei let his thoughts linger on the construction company and Ivan's offer. Nikolai had made good points about his future. At the gym, he would always be an employee. At the construction company, he could be the boss. There were strings attached to this offer though. Could he handle them?

A sudden vision of a three a.m. phone call from Kostya or Ten requesting cement and the keys to a site hit him. Could he really slide out of the bed he would share with Bianca—with his wife and the mother of his child—to answer that call? To help them destroy whatever evidence needed to be destroyed and hidden away forever? Could he come home and shower and slide back into bed as if nothing had happened?

Chilled by the thought, he drove to the upscale assisted living community where Bianca's mother currently lived. She would be moving soon. At their barbecue on Saturday evening, Bianca's mother had surprised them by announcing she had closed on a house she would share with her two widowed sisters. It sat in a master planned community meant for independent senior living. Situated on a golf course, it had shopping nearby and hospitals, too. He hoped she would be happy there.

When he reached the front door of her apartment, he knocked and stepped back so she could see him through the peep hole. He waited patiently, fully aware that she moved slowly on the prosthetic leg she was still getting used to, and listened carefully in case she called for help. A short time later, he was greeted by Mona Bradshaw's smiling face.

Even though she was puttering around her house, Bianca's mother was perfectly primped in white trousers and a red fluttery top. She wore gold bangles that jingled as she waved him inside. "Sergei! Come in, honey."

The way she always spoke so kindly made him feel warm toward her. Even though she had known what he was the first time he had shown up on her doorstep with Bianca, she had never judged him too harshly. She had accepted him as he was and looked for the goodness in him. He silently prayed she wouldn't throw him out on his ass once he confessed what he had done.

"How are you?"

"Good, good. You?"

"Very good," he said and closed the door behind him.

"Would you like something to drink? I was just about to have a glass of lemonade." She gestured for him to follow her. "Come into the kitchen with me."

He followed her into the kitchen and took a seat at the small dining table near the bay window. Always nervous about her balance, he sat on the very edge of the chair and tensed his muscles. He was ready to pounce at the first sign of tottering, but she showed him how well she was doing in her rehab by easily obtaining two glasses from a cabinet and the pitcher of cold lemonade from the refrigerator.

"Thank you." He accepted a glass from her and waited for her to sit and take a sip before having his first drink. He relished the sweet tartness and nervously licked his upper lip. "Bianca mentioned inviting you over for dinner tonight after your meeting."

"That sounds nice. I'd like that."

"Good."

"Are you coming with us to the meeting?" She eyed him in a way that convinced him this was a discussion she had had with Bianca.

Remembering the way he had completely screwed things up that morning, he gently turned down the invitation. "No, ma'am."

"That's okay. When you're ready..."

"Yes, ma'am."

Mona stared expectantly over her glass. He was reminded of how much Bianca favored her mother. Both women had perfected a strong gaze that made him want to squirm like a five-year-old who had been caught sneaking a treat.

"Honey," she said with a laugh, "you look like you're about to tell me that you broke my windshield with a baseball." She spoke carefully, emphasizing the syllables and gliding over the consonant sounds that still gave her trouble after her stroke. "Whatever it is, just spit it out."

He cleared his throat and sat up straighter. "I love Bianca."

She smiled tenderly. "I know you do."

"I'm probably not the sort of man you imagined her loving."

"No," she agreed, "but you're the one she wants. You love her. You make her happy. That's all I want for her." She leaned forward. "What do *you* want for Bianca?"

He thought of all the things he wanted for her. "I want to make her smile every day. I want her to know that she's loved and supported. I want to do whatever it takes to help her achieve her career dreams. I want her to feel protected and provided for in every way."

"Just her?" Mona asked the question with a knowing lilt to her voice, and he gulped nervously. Rolling her dark eyes, she huffed with laughter. "Sergei, I'm not blind. My daughter might have thought that she covered herself well when she excused herself from the barbecue, but I know morning sickness when I see it."

"It's my fault," he hurriedly said, desperate to deflect any blame from Bianca.

"Sweetheart, I've been a widow a long time, but I still remember how babies are made. There's enough blame to share equally."

"We want the baby. It's not the way it should have happened—"

"It rarely is," she sagely replied.

"I'm going to ask her to marry me. I would like to have your blessing. I think—I *know*—Bianca would like to have it."

"Of course she has it!" Mona looked surprised that there was any doubt. "I'm not thrilled about this situation. I raised Bianca to be more responsible. But," she emphasized the word, "I know she'll be a wonderful mother. I think you'll be a good husband and father. If..."

"If?" An invisible band squeezed his chest as he waited for her condition.

"If you're done with all that mess you were in when we first met," she stated.

"I am." He didn't give her the details. "It's done. That chapter of my life is finished." With a smile, he added, "The only boss I plan to serve is Bianca."

She laughed. "Sounds like a good plan, but I'll warn you. She's a tough boss to please."

"So I've learned."

With a pleased sigh, Mona gestured to his lemonade. "Finish that, and then you can take me to an early lunch. I have some errands I need to run, too. Also I'll need you to find some strong boys like yourself to help me when it's time to move."

Blinking with surprise, Sergei could only nod. He didn't dare tell her that he actually had plans for the rest of his day. The woman had just given him permission to marry her daughter and had reacted positively to the news that she was going to be a grandmother. "Yes, ma'am."

With a playful wink, she leaned forward and patted his hand. "Welcome to the family, Sergei."

Of all the things I expected to find when I pulled up to my mother's apartment that evening, Sergei toting shopping bags from the back of his SUV to my mother's front door wasn't one of them. I parked my car and slid out of the front seat just in time to hear Mama remarking on his muscles and all the ways she could put them to use. *Really?*

Sergei noticed me coming down the sidewalk and stopped to wait for me. That sexy smile of his made my belly do wild flips. He bent down to kiss me. Not wanting him to sneak away just yet, I tugged on the bottom of his shirt to keep him there a few seconds longer. When I finally let him go, he made sure to brush his lips against my forehead. "How are you feeling?"

"Fine." I noticed Mama had already gone into the house. "Just some nausea, but I managed to keep it under control."

"I'm glad to hear that." His hungry gaze moved over my outfit. The searing heat of it made my breasts ache. I squeezed my thighs together to ease the throbbing pulse there. "I think you wear these tight skirts to tease me."

"Well, you'd better enjoy them while you can." I rubbed his hard chest and enjoyed the feel of muscle definition beneath my fingertips. "My days of hip-hugging skirts are coming to a close."

A rumbling sound of dissent left his throat. He tilted his head to the side and studied my high heels. "What happened to wearing comfortable shoes?"

"These are comfortable." They were my roomiest pair of pumps with a sensible heel. "Mostly," I added as an afterthought. Before he could comment on my choice of footwear, I turned my attention to the bags he held. There was only one place that had all those stores under one roof. "Did she drag you to the Galleria?"

"She needed to run some errands."

Falling into step beside him, I insisted, "Shopping isn't such an important errand that she had to take you away from work."

"It was nice to spend the day with her." Despite the heavy bags burdening his arms, he still held the front door open for me and let me pass first.

Inside the apartment, I found my mother in the kitchen. "Mama, if you needed to go shopping, you should have asked me."

"I was going to ask you." She kissed my cheek in a greeting. "But Sergei came by for lunch so I asked him instead."

"Lunch?" I glanced back and forth between the pair. "You two had lunch?"

"We went to Luby's." He placed her bags on the table. "I had never been there. It was tasty."

I tried to imagine Sergei and my mother dining on chicken fried steak at Luby's. It was a comical picture, to say the least. "You've lived in Texas for more than five years, and you've never eaten at Luby's?"

He shrugged. "Now I have." He glanced at his watch. "I should go." He stepped toward me and gave me a quick kiss. "Dinner?"

I nodded. "We'll be home around eight."

Mama held out her arms for a hug, and Sergei obliged. "Thank you for humoring an old lady."

"It was no trouble. You have my number now. Call me if you need anything."

I waited until I heard the front door close to interrogate my mother. "Okay, what was *that* about?"

She brushed off my curiosity and started digging through her bags. "We had lunch. We shopped. It was no big deal."

"No big deal? Mama, you've never gone to lunch or shopped with any of my boyfriends."

"It's different with Sergei."

I had to hear this one. "Because?"

"Because he's the father of my grandbaby," she said matter-of-factly. Her coffee brown eyes almost dared me to deny it.

My emotions warred within me. Shock, fear, and the slightest twinge of betrayal surged through me. "He told you."

"Don't be too angry with him. He was trying to protect you."

Feeling like a little girl and on the verge of tears at the thought of disappointing my mother, I whispered, "I'm sorry, Mama."

Her face fell, and she opened her arms. "Sweetie, come here."

Safe in my mother's arms, I burrowed into her neck and let some of the fear I had been feeling since learning I was pregnant escape. "Mama, I don't know the first thing about having a baby."

"You'll learn," she assured me while soothingly rubbing my back. "You've got so much love in you. I'll be there with you." She hugged me tighter. "I'm always here for you."

"I never wanted to embarrass or disappoint you, Mama. You taught me to be smart and responsible but—"

"Baby, you could never disappoint me! After everything we've survived and all you've accomplished? No! You're the most amazing young woman I've ever known and I'm so proud to be your mother"

Her kind words made me cry even harder. I pulled back and wiped at the tears that had spilled onto my cheeks. "You're not angry?"

"Over a new baby in the family? Never!" She pushed my hair behind my shoulder. "You're a grown woman. I would have preferred that you had done things the right way but..." She smiled at me. "A baby," she whispered excitedly. "It's about time we started adding new members to this family instead of losing them."

Thinking of my father and brother saddened me. They wouldn't be there to greet this tiny life growing inside me. A drunk driver and an angry, hateful white supremacist had seen to that. After all the pain our family had known, Mama was right. It was nice to have a new life to celebrate.

"Go freshen up your face," she gently suggested. "We don't want to be late for our meeting."

"Yes, ma'am."

She touched me cheek. "It'll be all right, sugar. You'll see."

Because my mother said it, I knew it had to be true.

3 CHAPTER THREE

"No, you're putting emphasis on the wrong syllable."
Vivian leaned forward and drew lines under the word
she had spelled out phonetically for me. "Zuh-dras-voo-
tye. *Zdrastvutje.* Try again."

Sitting in the library of the grand historic home she
shared with her husband, I tried to concentrate on the
Russian lesson, but the imposing, intimidating man
hovering near the doorway interrupted my concentra-
tion. The man Vivi had earlier introduced as Ten
leaned against the doorframe now and watched us in
the most unnerving way. He didn't speak or smile. He
simply stared.

For some reason I couldn't fathom, Nikolai had chosen this terrifying beast to replace Sergei as his wife's bodyguard. Blond with the faintest reddish tint to his hair, Ten was shorter than Sergei but still very tall. His shoulders weren't nearly as broad either, but he was uncommonly muscular with thick arms and legs. The mean hands curled into loose fists had probably done some serious damage over the years.

He had more tattoos than I had ever seen in my life. Not even Ivan had as many as this man. Most of the ones on his neck and arms looked like prison ink with their rough, blurred edges and uneven coloring, but there was one tattoo—a bold, brightly hued tiger that stretched from the underside of his left wrist up above the crook of his elbow—that looked professionally done. I didn't even want to think about what those daggers with bloody tips or that creepy spider just visible inside the open collar of his shirt meant.

Vivi seemed to notice my discomfort. "Ten, you don't have to babysit me. When we're here at the house, you should make yourself comfortable."

"The boss said I'm supposed to keep both eyes on you."

Her lips pressed together, and I sensed that there was some friction between husband and wife over this issue. Gently and with more patience than I ever could have mustered, she explained, "You'll soon learn that

I'm the boss in this house. Right now, I want to be alone with my friend. You might like the media room?"

Ten still didn't move. In a rough and rasping voice, he meanly replied, "I don't take my orders from women."

My lips parted in shock at the outrageous way he spoke to her. *Is he insane?* I shivered to think what Nikolai would do when he found out this man had spoken to his wife in that tone.

Coolly and calmly, Vivian rose from her chair and crossed the library. Ten's jaw twitched as she drew near. His eyes were so dark they seemed nearly black and fathomless. She didn't show an ounce of fear as she grasped one of the belt loops on his jeans and tugged him toward the door. He fought her at first, but she pulled harder and he finally relented. When he was out in the hall, she pivoted on her heel, stepped back inside the library and shut the door in his face. As if to prove her point, she flipped the lock.

She took her seat and picked up her pen. Pointing at the Russian greeting, she said, "Let's try again. You've only got a few days until you meet Sergei's mother."

"Vivi! Forget about the lesson." I hooked my thumb toward the door. "That guy was a jerk!"

She reached for her cup of lukewarm peach-flavored tea and sipped at it. "This isn't easy for him. I never knew him before he went inside, but I've heard the stories. He was part of the inner circle and hugely respected. He's the sort of street soldier every other soldier wanted to be. He sacrificed himself to save the family—and now he's been rewarded with a babysitting job." She swirled her spoon in the cup. "I'm sure he feels slighted by the downgrade in his status."

"How in the world is protecting the one thing in the world Nikolai considers most precious a downgrade?"

"I'm sure Ten doesn't see it that way." She glanced at the door. "He's only been out of prison for two days. He needs some time to adjust to living on the outside again." She sighed wistfully. "He's no Sergei or Danny but he'll keep me safe. I enjoyed having someone to talk to but I don't need that sort of friendship from my bodyguard."

I doubted that very much. In fact, I suspected she very much needed the friendship Sergei and Danny had provided. "Why isn't Danny with you anymore?"

"He got a promotion." She wasn't going to give any further details, and I didn't push. I had gotten a glimpse into the shadowy world her husband inhabited and that was quite enough for me.

"So Ten, huh? What sort of nickname is that?"

"It's actually a bastardization of this word." She reached for the pen and neatly printed four Cyrillic letters—ТеbН. "It's pronounced *tyen.* It sounds like ten, and there's this rumor that he once iced ten men with his bare hands and a piece of pipe. Whether that's true or not...?" She shrugged her delicate shoulders. "It makes for a good story, I guess."

Somehow I didn't doubt that vicious-looking man had done far worse than what was rumored. I tapped the word she had written. "What does it mean?"

"Shadow."

"Oh."

"Yeah." She sat back and smiled. "It's funny because I used to joke with Sergei that he was my shadow. Now I have *the* Shadow following me around everywhere."

She said it like a joke, but I could hear the underlying frustration in her voice. "I'm sorry, Vivi."

She traced the letters neatly printed on the notebook page between us. "I knew what I was signing up for when I fell in love with Kolya. I definitely knew the score when we got married. Lena warned me I had to take him as he was, and I did."

"But?"

"But sometimes it's hard," she admitted quietly. "Not the loving him part," she clarified, "but the rest of it? That part isn't easy."

Certain she wasn't finished venting, I held my tongue and waited for her to speak again.

"Lena has been running interference as my PR rep for the upcoming show, and it's gotten dicey a few times. Journalists who cover the art scene want to dig around in our lives, and I can tell it's making Kolya uncomfortable. He's on edge already with all that mess in—" She stopped suddenly. "He's on edge because of work, and now he's got to worry about a journalist getting a little too close. He won't say that, of course. He acts like he's totally thrilled for me, but I can tell he's having second thoughts."

My eyes widened. "About?"

She didn't answer immediately. Her throat bobbed, and she blinked rapidly. "All of it. The art show. The business...compromises he's had to make. Me."

"Bullshit." I refused to believe that last part. "That's not possible. That man adores you. He loves you, Vivian. He's ice cold with everyone but you. Beyond the obvious, he doesn't strike me as the sort of man who makes big life decisions without thinking them through very carefully. He wanted you as his wife. He chose you knowing full well what that entailed."

She rubbed her face between her elegantly-boned hands. Her cuticles were stained with bright pigments.

"I feel like we're drifting, and I don't know how to close the gap."

Suddenly all the good news I had wanted to share with her turned sour in my belly. My heart ached for Vivi, and I didn't dare add to her misery by announcing that I was pregnant when she herself couldn't even reveal the news of her own impending bundle of joy. It struck me then how very lucky I was that Sergei was out of the mob. It had cost us both so much—in money and danger and more—but it was worth it.

Grasping her hand, I gave it a squeeze. "Make this London getaway into a vacation about the two of you. After your show, maybe you two can disappear for a few days. Even if you hole up in some hotel suite, it would be a good way for you to reconnect. You can pretend that none of this," I gestured around us, "exists. It will be just the two of you."

She nodded slowly. "I've been thinking the same thing. We never had a honeymoon. When we got married, it was too dangerous to go anywhere and now..." She sighed. "Well."

I wished more than anything that I was brave enough to ask her what was happening in the underworld that had everyone so nervous and on edge, but I was too afraid. I didn't want to know things that I shouldn't. I really, really didn't want to put myself or the baby growing inside me at risk.

"Anyway," she said with a long exhale. "Let's get back to this." She started jotting down new words on the notepad. "Sergei's brother speaks English so you'll be able to talk with him easily. His mother probably knows a little, but if you want to make a good impression, you should at least memorize these."

Over the next hour, she schooled me in the various phrases I might find useful. She had such patience with me, but I was absolutely terrible. For a girl fluent in French and Spanish, I couldn't get a handle on Sergei's language. Doubts started to creep in as I tried again and again to get it right. I had flashbacks to that awful run-in with Sergei's ex-girlfriend in the restroom at Samovar. All the nasty things she had snarled my way taunted me. Though Lidia and I had made peace, those seeds of doubt started to sprout.

Voices in the hallway interrupted our lesson. A moment later, someone tried to open the library door. Knuckles rapped loudly against the wood. "Vee!"

The irritation in Nikolai's voice surprised me. Rolling her eyes, Vivi exhaled a noisy breath and unfolded her legs from the tucked up position she had in her chair. She crossed the library, unlocked and opened the door. I kept my gaze fixed on the notepad in front of me while the couple argued behind me. The hissed whispers of Russian were foreign to my ears, but I didn't need to speak their language to understand that all was not well within the walls of this house.

Thinking of the many, many years the pair had been bound together as friends and something more before their marriage, I couldn't help but wonder about the relationship I had with Sergei. Our foundation was thinner and smaller. Were we going to start fighting like this? Did we have what it took to make a go of something real? Tossing a baby into a brand new relationship wasn't going to help matters any.

Twirling the pen between my fingers, I silently vowed to work hard at our relationship. It wasn't going to be easy. There were probably going to be days where I wanted to smack him with a broom or make him sleep downstairs, but I wasn't exactly sweet as pie myself. *Compromise. We'll have to learn to compromise.*

"Bianca, it's good to see you."

Twisting in my seat, I smiled at Nikolai. He wore a soft expression, but I could see the stress tightening his handsome features. Vivian had a gentle hand on his chest, and he covered it with his own. Their gazes met briefly, his apologetic and warm with his love for her, and I sensed the storm between them would soon pass.

"It's nice to see you, too." Certain the couple needed some time, I gathered up the notepad and my purse. I made a show of glancing at my watch. "I need to run. Sergei will be home soon. I promised to handle dinner tonight."

"What time are you two heading to the airport on Sunday?"

"I think Sergei said eight?" I tucked the notepad into my purse along with the capped pen. "What about you two?"

"Eight," Nikolai answered. "You're staying at the same hotel as Erin and Ivan?"

"Yes."

"And Sergei's mother and brother are joining us on Tuesday evening?"

I nodded. "They'll be with us until Sunday morning when they fly back to Russia."

"I haven't had a chance to talk with Sergei about the immigration situation. It's going well?"

"He had a meeting with his new lawyer earlier this week. It seems promising so far." While Sergei had permanent resident status, his mother and brother had been trying unsuccessfully to join him in Houston. After an unscrupulous lawyer had cheated dozens of immigration hopefuls out of their hard-earned money, Sergei had been forced to start the process all over again for his family. Now we were working with an attorney recommended by Nikolai and Yuri Novakovsky, the billionaire tycoon who seemed to have a Rolodex stuffed to the brim with useful contacts.

"I'm glad to hear that. It will be good for the entire family to be here together."

"Yes, it will." Sergei and I were happy, but I understood how much he missed his mother and brother. They were all he had left of his family, and they needed to be here with him. *With us.*

"Ten?" Nikolai slid his arm around Vivian's shoulders and guided her to one side of the doorway. The intimidating ex-con stepped into view but said nothing. He simply waited for his instruction. "Walk Bianca out to her car."

"*Da.*"

"Oh, I don't need an escort," I said with a light laugh. The thought of being alone with Ten in the dark made my knees knock together. "I'm a big girl."

"It's no trouble." Nikolai's gaze was kind, but I understood this wasn't up for debate. "I insist."

Thinking of the last time I had left his house after dark and run into Detective Eric Santos, I wondered if there wasn't some truly serious reason he didn't want me traipsing around outside alone. My concern for Vivian skyrocketed. *What the hell was going on out there?* More than anything, I was so damned happy Sergei was out of this life. We didn't have to look over our shoulders anymore. We were free.

Vivian walked me to the front door, and we exchanged quick hugs while Ten waited on the front porch. Walking next to him in the darkness, I was taken aback by how silently he moved. I began to form a better picture of why they called him the Shadow.

While Sergei put others at ease with that boyish grin of his, Ten seemed to have a permanent scowl twisting his mouth. Where Sergei hated for others to fear him simply because of his size, Ten relished it. He wanted me to be afraid of him. He wanted me to scurry along like some terrified little girl—but I refused to be cowed.

"So how is life on the outside treating you?"

Ten actually snorted. It wasn't a sound of derision though. It was amusement. "Yeah," he said finally. "It's okay. Besian's dancing girls have been fun."

I glanced over at him and caught the tail end of a smirk on his face. He probably expected me to get huffy at him talking about strippers, but I didn't take the bait. "Yes, I hear that Sugar's and Wet are some of the better establishments in the city, if that's your preference for entertainment."

"My preference is for something in a different class, but I'll make do." There was no mistaking the heated gaze that settled on my breasts and then my hips. The summery dress I had chosen that morning had a vintage flare to it with a sweetheart neckline and a flirty red skirt with tiny white polka dots. It was one of Sergei's favorites, and he had spent a few minutes nuzzling into my cleavage before running out the door. Judging by Ten's lingering leer, he was having the same idea.

Snapping my fingers, I pointed to my face. "My eyes are up here. This," I gestured to my bosom, "belongs to someone else. You'd better remember that the next time you see me."

"I was inside for six years. You can't blame a man for looking when the view is that nice."

"Well, thank you for the compliment, but—"

"Yeah," he cut me off. "You're his." As we drew near my car, he added, "You chose well. Sergei will take care of you. He'll keep you safe from those lightning bolt shitheads."

Ten's words sent a quiver of panic through me. "That's done. Everything with Adam Blake is over." Naming my brother's killer no longer affected me in the way it once had.

"It's never over, girl. Darren Blake is gone. Adam Blake is wasting away in a prison infirmary, but it's not *over*. There are others. There will always be others." He looked down at me as if I might be the stupidest woman he had ever met. "Don't tell me you thought the two of you were going to ride off into the fucking sunset like a pair of lovers from some fairy tale."

"No," I insisted angrily, but obviously I had thought that. "Of course, I didn't think that."

"Good," he shot back. "Because it doesn't work like that. Sergei bled for this family. He made others bleed for this family. That doesn't wash off, understand?"

No, not really. But I lied nonetheless. "Yes."

Shaking his head, he reached for my door handle but didn't open it. Putting his massive hand on the roof of my car, Ten pinned me in place with a look that was equal parts pitying and frustrated. "The boss and his wife? They like you too much to upset you, but I don't have that problem. So I'm going to be straight with you. All that studying you're doing to impress your *svekrov*? It won't work."

I recognized the word as the one used for a mother-in-law. Swallowing nervously, I asked, "Why?"

"Why?" He repeated with a harsh chortle. I jerked back when he reached for my hand, but he held tight and forced my hand into the shaft of light illuminating us from the streetlamps. "This is why."

At first I didn't understand, but then his callused thumb rubbed a circle on my skin. It was a painful and ugly thought that I refused to accept. "You don't even know Sergei or his family."

"I don't have to know them to know how this is going to play out once you meet them." His thumb moved side to side over the back of my hand. "You're beautiful. You're smart. You have a career and a successful business. You think your stock is pretty high, right? But you're wrong. You're not the sort of woman his mother wants for her *nevestka*."

"You're an asshole." I yanked free from him and shoved his hand off my car.

Ten put his hand against the door and kept me from opening it. That terrifying tiger stretched across his arm snarled at me. "Yes, I am, but I'm honest. I wouldn't lie to you, not about something like this."

I studied his face. Scary as he was, I could see he was earnest. "Why?"

His gaze unsettled me. "I know a good person when I see them. I don't come across them often, but I can tell you're one of them. You love your man, and he loves you enough to leave all of this," he twirled his finger in the air, "behind. There's only one woman in the world who can take that from you."

My stomach dropped. "His mother."

Ten nodded. "That's a bond that you will never break. So you had better make your war plan now, girl. You put on that armor, and you make sure she knows that you faced off with Nikolai Fucking Kalasnikov to save her son. *You* did that. *You* gave her back the son she had lost. Make her remember who she owes her happiness to—and then you win."

"It won't be that easy."

"No, it won't." He lifted his hand and reached for my door handle. "But something tells me you're not easily beaten." He held the door open for me. "Good luck, Bianca."

"Thank you." Reeling from our bizarre conversation, I slipped into the driver's seat and dropped my purse on the passenger side. Ten stood on the sidewalk until I disappeared around the corner. I tried to make sense of the mysterious, intimidating man. He had nothing to gain from helping me, yet he had done it anyway. I took that as a good sign as far as Vivian's safety went. Ten was far from nice, but honesty, loyalty, and honor more than made up for that.

When I reached the house, I pulled through the gate at the back of my property and into the space next to Sergei's SUV. With my purse in one hand, I bumped my car door closed and waited for the lights to blink and the horn to blip before I headed up the sidewalk to the back entrance through the screened porch and sunroom. The door leading into the house opened with a squeak, and Sergei appeared, his huge frame silhouetted by the light from the mudroom.

"Hey." I smiled at him as I drew near and let my needy gaze roam his bare chest and the khaki cargo shorts that sat dangerously low on his hips.

Sergei swooped down and kissed me when I was close enough. Just as I had expected, his lips traveled down my neck to the swell of cleavage displayed by the neckline of my dress. He nuzzled my breasts and placed noisy kisses on my throbbing flesh. "I missed you."

"You missed me or the girls?" I playfully asked.

"Both," he murmured before pressing his lips to my cheek. "I grabbed Chinese for dinner. I hope that's okay."

"It was my turn to cook," I reminded him as I pushed by him and into the house.

"Was it?"

I knew he hadn't forgotten. No doubt he had convinced himself I would be too tired to make us dinner. He seemed to think that being pregnant meant I should be sitting with my feet up as many hours in the day as possible.

"How is Vivi?" I hesitated answering him a moment too long. "Bianca? What's wrong with Vivian?"

I dropped my purse on the table and stepped out of my heels. "I think Vivian and Nikolai are having problems."

"Problems?"

"Marital problems," I clarified. "They argued while I was there."

"Lots of couples argue."

"True, but she said that she feels like they're drifting apart. I could tell she wanted to talk, but she didn't want to share too much with me because of...well...you know."

"Yes," he said sadly.

"And now she's got this freaking terrifying body-guard named Ten," I continued. "He's not like you. He was really rude to her, and then he walked me out to my car—"

"Wait." Sergei held up one of his massive hands. "You were alone with Ten?"

"Yes."

Sergei's jaw clenched. He closed the distance between us and started to look me over as if he expected to find bruises on my body. "Did he hurt you?"

"Hurt me?" I reared back with surprise. "He was a jerk, but he wasn't mean. He treated me with respect." I decided to leave out the part about Ten ogling me. With a nervous gulp, I added, "He gave me some advice on dealing with your mother."

"He *what*?" Sergei's nostrils flared. He cursed in Russian and shook his head. "Whatever he told you? Forget it. That man knows nothing about my family or us. He's not the sort of man you should be spending time with alone."

"Why?" I couldn't wrap my head around Sergei's reaction to Ten. "Nikolai trusts him to guard Vivian."

"Because the boss knows Ten is an animal who will kill without a moment's hesitation," Sergei snapped.

Blowing out a noisy breath, he placed his hands on my shoulders and slid them toward my neck. Cupping my face, he held my gaze and entreated me to listen carefully. "You know what I am, Bianca. You know what I've done for the family, but I never, *never*, took pleasure in it."

"I know that," I whispered. "I know you're not like that."

His thumbs glided along my cheeks. "Ten is a loyal man. He has honor, but he also has a taste for blood. He did things..." Sergei couldn't even bring himself to talk about them. "I don't want you spending time alone with him."

"All right." I bit my lower lip. "But when I'm with Vivi?"

"When you're with her, it's fine. He'll keep the two of you out of trouble, but I don't want you walking around alone with him. Six years is a long fucking time for a man to go without his favorite thing." Sergei looked me up and down. "And you are precisely what he likes."

My eyes widened at that. "What? Big girls? Black girls?"

"Both," he said. "You are exactly the kind of girl he used to chase."

"Oh." Suddenly the way Ten had held my hand and traced his thumb over my skin felt less than innocent.

Perhaps he had been motivated to warn me about the possibility of Sergei's mother disliking me for other reasons. Was he interested in me? That was all I needed! An ex-con with the hots for me!

Glancing up at Sergei, I spotted the briefest glimmer of vulnerability on his face. "Are you seriously worried that I would choose someone like that over you?"

"No."

"But?"

"But he's got a reputation for taking things that don't belong to him."

Huffing, I thumped his chest. "I'm not a possession."

"You're mine," he reminded me in that alpha way he somehow made so endearing. "You belong to me just as I belong to you."

Ten's warning about Sergei's mother echoed in my head. "And what if other people think we shouldn't belong to each other?"

"Fuck those other people," he stated passionately. "No one is going to keep me from you."

"Not even your mother?" I asked in a small voice.

His eyes narrowed. "Is that what Ten told you? That my mother doesn't want us together?"

"He told me that she might not like me."

Sergei's cheek twitched and his lips settled into a grim line. "Even if that were true, I wouldn't stop loving you. I wouldn't walk away from you or the baby. I'm a grown man, and I've chosen you. I would like to have my family's support, but I don't need it." One of his hands cupped the back of my neck while the other settled on my belly. "I have everything I need right here."

His reassurances settled my nerves. Whatever happened in London, we wouldn't let it break us apart. We had made it through so much in such a short span of time. We could make it through his mother's disapproval if it came to that.

Smiling down at me, he asked, "How did your lesson go?"

I pouted. "I'm terrible, Sergei. You would think after all those years of French and Spanish, I would be able to pick up a new language easily, but it's not happening."

"It's a different type of language. You could probably learn Portuguese or Italian without too much trouble, but Russian? It's more complicated."

"It's the sounds. My tongue refuses to do the right thing."

"Does it?" His sexy mouth curved in playful way. "I happen to know some very good tongue exercises you could try."

Now I was the one grinning. "Oh, really?"

"Mmmhmm," he rumbled and ran his finger along the top of my breast. "In fact, I could show you right now."

"Or," I let my hands fall to the waistband of his cargo shorts, "I could show you."

"Bianca," he breathed my name as I lowered myself to the floor. Kneeling at his feet, I made quick work of unbuttoning and unzipping his cargo shorts. I tugged down his boxers and freed his cock. Half hard and already more impressive than most men, his shaft enthralled me. I licked my lips and fondled him gently. My fingertips stroked the length of him, my touch light but firm.

When I flicked my tongue against the underside of the blunt tip, he reached back to grip the counter. Smirking at the way I could so easily overwhelm this powerful giant, I swirled my tongue around the head of his cock and then slowly sucked him between my lips. He was so thick that he stretched my mouth wide, and I loved it. He was too long for me to take all of him. Maybe someday I would work up to that, but I didn't have the skills yet.

Not that he minded at all. Sergei held perfectly still as I bobbed on his shaft, taking him deeper and twirling my tongue around the crown of him. The groans that erupted from his chest made my clit pulse. I

sucked him harder and faster, giving him exactly what
he needed. I could taste the slight sweetness of his pre-
cum spilling onto my tongue now. He was getting
close.

"Bianca." He growled like a bear.

I put my hands on his thighs and felt his muscles
tensing under my palms. I leaned forward and relaxed
my jaw, taking as much of his rock-hard length as I
could. He gripped my hair in his hands, settling them
on either side of my face, and gently thrust against my
tongue. "Look at me," he urged, his voice husky. "Look
at me while you suck my cock."

Our gazes clashed. He panted now, his chest heav-
ing and his stomach caving in with each breath. I
moaned around the cock gliding in and out of my
mouth, and he came with a roar. Frozen like a statue,
he let me take over again, let me bob and flick and
swallow burst after burst of his cum until he finally
collapsed back against the counter on shaking legs.

Like a lion pouncing on prey, he stunned me with a
flash of movement. Before I knew what was happening,
he had me flat on my back on the floor. Not caring
about the shorts hanging low on his thighs, he shoved
my legs apart, jerked my skirt up around my hips and
yanked on my panties. The fabric ripped as he tore
them down my legs and tossed them over his shoulders.

Showing how gentle he could be even when frantic for me, Sergei caressed my face and whispered sweetly to me in Russian. He claimed my mouth in a possessive, passionate kiss. His tongue stabbed against mine, swiping my teeth and the roof of my mouth. Sergei's rough, hot hand rode the curve of my waist to glide down my leg and cup my bottom. He squeezed my aching flesh and nipped at my throat before palming my throbbing pussy in his big hand.

"Sergei..."

Chuckling against my skin, he whispered, "I want to hear you sing."

A quiver of anticipation rocked my belly at the teasing words he used to describe the way I cried out when I approached an orgasm. His thick, skilled fingers parted the most delicate part of me and slid in the slickness there. He groaned when he learned how wet I was for him. His thumb circled my clit a few times, and I gasped at the sharp sensation.

Easing off, he plunged two fingers into my slit, working them up into me and curving them at just the right angle. He pumped into me, touching that spot inside my pussy that made my entire body seize with pleasure. His thumb returned to my clit. He strummed that little pearl until I was clawing at his shoulders and begging him for release. "Please. *Please.*"

"Come on," he urged gruffly. "Come, Bianca. *Come.*"

The vibrations of his wickedly deep voice set me off like a bottle rocket on the Fourth of July. Clutching his arm, I lifted my hips, pressing my pussy to that sinful hand of his, and let loose a wild cry of pleasure. Higher and higher in octave, my voice echoed off the ceiling.

"*Da*," he said with a smile in his voice. "*More*. Sing, Bianca."

His hand moved faster now, his fingers slamming into my wet sheath with such speed that there was no holding back. I surrendered to the incredible sensations he evoked. When he went into alpha lover mode like this, there was nothing to do but submit and trust. I closed my eyes and welcomed wave after rapturous wave.

"I need you," he growled and shoved between my thighs. He was hard again. I didn't know how that was possible, but somehow, some way, he always was. *For me.* He grasped the base of his wide shaft and dragged the ruddy head through my lower lips, gathering my wetness on his skin before lining up and thrusting into me. "Yes."

Using his brute strength, he clasped my waist and canted my hips to a higher angle. He took me with long, hard thrusts that left me babbling like a fool.

Panting, shuddering and slapping at the tile floor, I writhed under his huge body. I peered up at Sergei— *my* Sergei—and grinned. There was no other man in the world who could make fucking on the kitchen floor seem so special.

Because he's with me.

And that was the truth of it. When we were together, everything was special. Everything was perfect. As dinner cooled on the counter and the sounds of our lovemaking filled the house, I couldn't imagine a better way to end our day.

4 CHAPTER FOUR

"Did you pack your entire closet?" Sergei teased Bianca as he hefted one of her suitcases out of the back of his SUV. He wasn't entirely joking though. The thing probably weighed sixty or seventy pounds.

"I didn't hear you complaining when you were hauling Mama's shopping bags around," she replied while pushing her sunglasses into place. "You better not let Ivan hear you whining. He'll probably have you doing push-ups all the way across the Atlantic."

Laughing, Sergei grabbed her smaller suitcase and set it between the two larger ones. He extended the handle and let her take it with some reluctance. In the back of his mind, he knew that he was overreacting when it came to Bianca carrying things or pulling her smaller, much lighter rolling suitcase, but he couldn't help himself. That positive pregnancy test had ignited every protective male instinct within him.

Scanning the parking lot, he discovered a familiar vehicle parked close to the terminal. It was one of the SUVs from Nikolai's fleet. There was one man sitting in the driver's seat. Boychenko, he realized, when the younger man waved once. Lifting his hand, Sergei suspected the other guard—Ten—sat inside the building with Vivian.

"This will be fun." Bianca smiled excitedly as they crossed the parking lot to the terminal of the executive airport. "We get to see how the one-percent live."

He chuckled at her enthusiasm. With any other woman, he might secretly fear that she would impressed by the luxury a man like Yuri Novakovsky could provide and want more of that, but he knew enough about Bianca's spending habits and life outlook to be sure that wasn't the case. From what he had witnessed between Yuri and his girlfriend, Lena didn't much care about the money either. It was probably the reason Yuri loved her so much. She never asked for or expected anything but his love and emotional support.

A skycap met them on the sidewalk and took their bags. Bianca checked her purse for the hundredth time to be sure their passports were in there before she let the man head off with their luggage. When they stepped inside the bright, airy terminal, Sergei tugged off his aviator sunglasses and tucked them into his pocket. His gaze immediately landed on Ten who stood just inside the entrance.

Arms crossed, he wore a blazer that covered the prison and gang ink Sergei knew colored his skin. No doubt that had been at Vivian's insistence. He and Ten shared a long look, one that was wary but respectful. When Ten's interested gaze fell on Bianca, he swallowed the growl that threatened to erupt from his throat and the alpha need to show possessiveness toward her. She wouldn't like it, and he was determined not to upset her this early in their vacation.

Ignoring Ten, he eased Bianca farther into the terminal. He spotted Vivian, Erin and Lena sitting in leather chairs off to the left. Two of them were chatting and laughing, but Vivian checked her watch and stared at the entrance. When she noticed him looking at her, she smiled thinly.

"I'll be with the girls." Bianca gave his arm a squeeze and started to move away, but he caught her hand and dragged her back for a quick kiss. He liked the way she blushed and enjoyed the view of her curvy hips swinging as she joined her friends. He didn't think a pair of white capris had ever looked that fucking good on any woman.

But she's not any woman. She's my *woman.* The thought filled him with heat. Soon, he would make sure that she really was his. She would share his name and wear his wedding band and everyone would know that he was the luckiest fucking man in the world.

A quick glance around the terminal, and he found Ivan and Yuri talking nearby. As he drew near, he noticed both men looked worried. He didn't know Yuri that well but the billionaire businessman had always treated him like a friend. Even so, he made sure to approach slowly, just in case the pair needed to wrap up their discussion without him overhearing any of it.

Yuri was the first to welcome him with a handshake and a warm smile. "You're looking much better than the last time I saw you."

Considering the oligarch had last seen him after two nights of fighting in a cage, Sergei believed it. "It's good to see you again."

Ivan clapped him on the back. "Are you excited to see your family?"

He couldn't stop the grin that pulled at the corners of his mouth. "Yes."

"How long has it been?" Yuri asked.

"Five and a half years," Sergei said. Actually, he could tell Yuri down the very minute he had stepped onto that plane in the middle of a cold Moscow night, but he didn't. "It feels longer."

Ivan squeezed his shoulder and exchanged a glance with Yuri. Stepping closer and lowering his voice, he said, "Listen, there's a problem."

Ears perked, Sergei frowned. "With?"

"Vivian."

He fought the urge to look back at her. "What sort of problem?"

"Nikolai called me a few minutes ago," Yuri explained. "He can't get out of the...*meeting*...he's in so he's going to miss our flight. I offered to hold the jet but he told us to go."

Sergei's chest tightened. If the boss was missing something this huge, it had to be serious. Being out of the loop suddenly didn't feel so freeing. Not knowing what was happening on the shadowy streets of Houston's underworld made him nervous. "Have you told her yet?"

"We were about to tell her. He didn't want Ten to be the one to do it." Yuri frowned at the ex-con guarding Vivian. "I can see why."

"I'll go," Ivan offered.

Sergei shook his head. "I'll tell her. She's used to hearing this sort of news from me."

He didn't miss the sad looks the two friends exchanged as he left them. In the months he had spent constantly at her side as her bodyguard, they had established a relationship that resembled that of siblings. He had learned how to let her down easily. *Don't make her cry.* He repeated the words to himself as he sat down next to her.

Vivian's bright blue eyes fixed on his. Long seconds stretched between them as they stared at one another. Finally, in softly spoken Russian, she whispered, "He's not coming."

Sergei's heart fucking shattered in his chest. A memory came to him of the morning Vivian had woken to an empty house after spending her wedding night alone. Instead of the beautiful, romantic breakfast she had envisioned, there had been only her bodyguard waiting for her. She had cried that morning, and he had been so angry with the boss for putting the family before her. It was an irrational thing to feel. Nikolai hadn't put her second because he didn't love her. He had put her needs behind those of the family because he *did* love her and he had been trying to keep her safe.

"If he could be here," Sergei said gently, but she didn't let him finish.

"I know." Resignation darkened her voice. Her eyes turned so cold that he felt the iciness deep in his soul. Plastering a fake smile into place, she grabbed the leather messenger bag she loved so much. "Tell Yuri we're ready to go. London's calling."

His stomach twisted as he realized that she was changing—and not for the better. The idea that there might not be a happy ending for the couple whose lives had seemed fated to cross left him feeling hollow and raw. He had never wanted to hold and kiss Bianca more.

Never, he swore silently as he returned to Yuri and Ivan. *I will never make Bianca feel like that. I will never let her doubt her importance to me.*

He noticed the curious looks the women exchanged as they realized Nikolai wasn't coming with them on this leg of the journey. Yuri muttered under his breath as they made their way to the jet waiting on the tarmac. Sergei didn't hear all of it, but what he did catch assured him that Nikolai would be getting an earful from his friend once he finally made his way to London.

Ten lingered on the tarmac until he saw Vivian disappear into the plane. Sergei had to give credit where it was due. He might be rough around the edges, but Ten was taking good care of Vivian. If it hadn't been for the travel restrictions that were part of his release, Ten probably would have gone with them.

When they settled into their plush seats aboard one of Yuri's private jets, Sergei reached for Bianca's hand

and interlaced their fingers. He couldn't see Vivian from their position in the cabin, and he wondered if he should let Bianca go sit with her. As if reading his mind, Bianca squeezed his hand and shook her head. "She wants to be alone."

"Not for the entire flight," he murmured.

"No," she agreed. "We'll take care of her. Don't worry."

"I can't help it. It was my job to worry about her. I can't simply turn that off."

She lifted their joined hands and kissed the back of his. "That's because you're a good man."

Holding her gaze, he said, "Bianca, if I ever make you feel—"

"You'll know it," she promised with a wicked gleam in her eye.

Glad they were on the same page, he chuckled softly and leaned back against the surprisingly roomy seat. The last time he had flown across the Atlantic, he had been stuffed into a coach seat. Thankfully he had been able to grab a spot in an exit row, but even that extra bit of leg room had barely made the flight tolerable. Tonight would be different.

Bianca's quip about living like the one-percent proved true. After takeoff, an incredible meal was served. Flight attendants catered to their every need. The bathrooms were three or four times the size of the ones found on commercial flights. Once dinner was finished, he settled into a section of the plane modeled after a media room to watch a baseball game with Yuri and Ivan.

His gaze skipped toward the front of the aircraft every now and then to check on Bianca and Vivian. The women were sitting together playing poker. By the size of the stacks of chips in front of her, Lena was winning every round. Vivian seemed to be in second place and Bianca wasn't far behind in third. Poor Erin had a tiny stack of chips left.

On his way to grab a bottle of water, Ivan seemed to notice the sad state of Erin's game. Taking pity on her, he crouched down beside her and slid an arm around her waist, hauling her closer so he could study her cards. He nuzzled her neck and whispered strategy in her ear.

Or maybe not strategy, Sergei thought with some amusement as Erin's ears and neck flushed a scarlet shade. Later that evening, when they reclined in their seats under warm blankets and caught some much needed sleep, he pretended not to notice when Erin first left her seat to use the restroom and then Ivan a few minutes later. He didn't blame Ivan one bite for wanting to cross that one off his bucket list. When the couple returned a long time later, he smirked knowingly and burrowed down deeper under his blanket.

They landed early the next morning to a surprisingly sunny and beautiful London day. Yuri had taken care of all the transportation arrangements. After clearing customs, they were whisked away from the airport to the oligarch's outrageously opulent Knightsbridge penthouse that spanned the top floor of a historic mansion. When they had been planning their trip, Bianca had mentioned that Yuri's London home was nearly ten thousand square feet of prime real estate. He couldn't even begin to comprehend how pricey that must have been. Tens of millions of pounds, he was sure.

But it was beautiful. The Victorian era mansion had been restored to period detail on the outside but the interior was a different story. The penthouse apartment had been redone with clean modern lines and open, bright spaces. There was a quarry's worth of white and black marble across the six bedrooms and seven bathrooms. He didn't particularly care for the interior design choices that had been made, but he could appreciate the way the space flowed from one room to the next.

As they enjoyed breakfast on the rooftop terrace, he thought of Bianca's Queen Anne home and the improvements they were making during the slow restoration process. She had wanted to stay true to the home's origins, and he agreed with that. The master bathroom they had recently completed was true to the period with modern tweaks.

He suddenly thought of the nursery they would soon have to decorate. He assumed they would turn the guest room next door to the master suite into their baby's room. Thinking of the wall that existed between the rooms, he wondered if a door might be possible there. It would make it easier to reach the baby in the middle of the night. As overprotective as he was with Bianca, he was probably going to be a nervous wreck once they had a baby in the house. To have an open door between their bed and the crib might be the best thing for his nerves.

When he caught Bianca yawning after breakfast, he thanked Yuri and Lena for their hospitality and excused them from the activities the other couples and Vivian had planned for their first day in London. Traveling across time zones was hard enough without being pregnant. Safely tucked into the back seat of a cab, he slid his arm around Bianca's shoulders and kissed her temple. "Why don't we spend the rest of the day in bed?"

She shot him a mischievous smile. "Knowing you, I doubt I'll get much sleep."

He drew an X over his heart. "I promise I'll be a good boy and keep my hands to myself."

She ran her hand up along the denim covering his thigh and came dangerously close to touching his cock. "Not too good of a boy, I hope."

With a low growl, he warned her not to test him in the back seat of the cab. She smirked and kept her hand right there, just inches from the throbbing heat trapped behind denim. By the time they reached the hotel, he was fucking aching for her. Somehow he managed to force down his erection so he could actually get out of the cab and oversee the transfer of their luggage from the cab to the bellhop's trolley. Once inside the lobby, Bianca handled their check-in.

He stood behind her, silently observing the bustling scene surrounding them. While she requested extra keys for his mother and brother who would be joining them the next day, Sergei heard the happy squeals of two young children. They seemed out of place in the lobby of the four-star hotel, and he zeroed in on the grinning, sticky faces of two preschool aged girls darting in and out of the crowd. They were cute kids.

My baby will look like that. The thought hit him right in the stomach, knocking the air from his lungs. The little girls were mixed race with skin like honey and dark curly hair pulled into pigtails that bounced as they ran circles around a column. Their harried mother, a thirty-something blonde, finally caught up with them, but it was their smiling father, a man who could have easily been part of Bianca's family, who swung them up in his arms and playfully nibbled at their necks.

"You okay?" Bianca rubbed his arm and drew him out of his thoughts. Her gaze settled on the family that gave them a glimpse at their future. Smiling, she said, "Cute."

"Very," he agreed and slid his arm around her back. Side by side, they walked to the elevator with the bellhop not far behind. If they had been alone in the elevator, he would have pushed her up against the gleaming gold wall and pressed his knee between her thighs while ravishing her mouth. Seeing the family that resembled theirs had done something primal to him. If she hadn't already been pregnant, he damned well would have wanted to change that.

On edge and fueled with lust, he barely managed to hold onto his patience while the bellhop unloaded their bags. He shoved a handful of foreign notes at the man and thanked him before herding him out the door and locking it behind him. By the time he found Bianca in the bedroom, she had already stripped down to her bra and panties.

"You know," she said slowly, her movements vixen-ish and enticing, "it occurred to me when I saw that family down in the lobby that this is probably the only vacation we'll ever take without kids."

Awestruck by the delicious sight before him, Sergei stood perfectly still and watched her reach back to unsnap her bra. When her luscious breasts were bared to him, he raked his teeth against his lower lip. After quickly toeing off his shoes, he crossed the distance between them in five quick strides and swept her up into his arms. He deposited her onto the middle of the fancy hotel bed and crawled over her.

In between kisses that left her breathless and giggling, he said, "Then we had better make the most of it..."

5 CHAPTER FIVE

My stomach did wild flips as I tried to pay attention to the movie. I couldn't tell if it was morning sickness or nervousness. It was probably both. The jet lag had worsened my pregnancy fatigue and made me more queasy than usual. So far, I'd managed to keep our secret, but I had a feeling the truth was going to be out before the end of this trip. One whiff of stinky perfume or cologne at the wrong time, and all of our friends would piece together the clues when I went running from the room.

Hugging a throw pillow, Vivian sat next to me on the couch in the hotel suite while we waited for Sergei to return from the airport with his brother and mother. She had said that she wanted to be here for moral support and to help with any translation issues that might arise if Sergei and Vladimir wanted to talk alone and leave me with his mother, but I sensed she really just didn't want to be the third wheel at Yuri and Lena's place. Not that they ever would have made her feel that way, but it couldn't have been easy for her.

Nikolai still hadn't made it to London. Even Sergei didn't know the details of what was keeping him in Houston. Whatever it was, it must have been serious—or dangerous—or dangerously serious. I hadn't had the heart to ask Vivian if her husband would be here in time for her Friday night show. I hoped so. For her sake and his.

"Do you want to grab lunch tomorrow? I was thinking of visiting some shops and seeing some of the fashion hotspots while Sergei does some things with his family."

She shook her head and picked at the fringe on the throw pillow. "I would love to go, but I've already promised Niels that I'd let him take me to some art galleries and a late lunch."

"Oh." I wondered if that was such a good idea. Vivian was obviously feeling vulnerable and hurt right now, and Niels? Well, the obscenely rich Dane who had taken it upon himself to open doors into the international art scene for her had made it plainly clear to anyone with eyes that he wasn't just interested in her paintings. She played it off as nothing, and I'm sure to her it was. She loved Nikolai and probably couldn't fathom ever entertaining the affection of another man, but Niels? He had a certain reputation, and it made me nervous to think my emotionally wounded friend would be alone with him for any amount of time.

"Why don't we do something on Thursday?" she suggested. "Maybe we could see if Lena and Erin want to come?"

"Sure. That sounds nice."

"I'll call them tomorrow and make arrangements."

We were talking about some of the shops we wanted to visit when the door of the suite beeped twice and started to open. I practically jumped to my feet. Anxiety rushed through me, made my belly lurch and my chest tighten. Rising more slowly, Vivian stood next to me and gently clasped my hand. She pumped my fingers with hers and winked reassuringly. I relaxed at the knowledge that she would guide me through this first meeting with Sergei's mother.

A man who could have been Sergei's twin sauntered through the door carrying small wrapped gifts. He shared the same dark hair and dark eyes and the giant frame of his elder brother. His friendly grin immediately set me at ease. There was a telltale bump in his nose that told me it had been broken, probably more than once. Apparently fighting was in the Sakharov family's blood.

The woman who followed Vladimir was shorter than I had expected. I had seen photos of Galina Sakharovna, of course, but Vladimir and Sergei had always been sitting on either side of her. She shared their dark hair and eyes but had a much lighter, willowy build. This close, I realized she was younger than my mother, which surprised me considering her children were all older. Like Mama, she had a flair for style and looked perfectly coiffed and dressed despite the four hour flight.

A faint smile curved Galina's bright red mouth. Vivian had warned me that customs were different between our two cultures. Unlike Mama, Sergei's mother wasn't going to call me honey and welcome me with a hug and sweet tea. The smile she cast my way wasn't much, but I figured it was a start, however shaky.

Radiating happiness, Sergei swept into the living room and gathered me close with a brawny arm. In a whirlwind of introductions, I was enveloped in a bear hug by Vladimir. He kissed both my cheeks and said something in rapid fire Russian that I couldn't understand. As if sensing my confusion, he said, "You're even prettier than Sergei described."

"Oh." I blushed. "Thank you."

He handed me one of the wrapped gifts. "I think you'll like these."

"I'm sure I will." The box wasn't very heavy, and it was the right size for chocolates or candy.

He stepped aside to greet Vivian with more reserve. She air-kissed his cheeks and spoke softly to him. He presented her with the other box, and she thanked him.

Sergei's mother stepped forward and tepidly embraced me. Galina gazed upon my face and smiled more warmly. "Yes. Very pretty."

"*Spasibo.*"

Her expression softened, but she turned her attention to Vivian now. I didn't miss the way his mother seemed to practically beam as Vivian chatted her up. I envied the easy way they spoke but hoped that in time she might see me the same way. After everything Lidia and Ten had warned me about, meeting his mother hadn't been nearly as awkward or upsetting as I had expected.

The room service order I had arranged arrived not long after Sergei and his family. We all sat down in the dining area of the suite and enjoyed a nice dinner. Vivian and I sat on either side of Galina, and Vivi jumped in to translate whenever necessary.

"Your dress shop is busy?" Galina pushed her spoon through the creamy custard flecked with bits of saffron. Considering we both worked in the same field, me a designer and her a seamstress, I wasn't surprised she asked after something we could both understand. Hopefully we might even bond over it.

"Yes, ma'am. We have a minimum of four bridal consultants on the floor every day. They take six to eight appointments each. We sold just over six thousand dresses last year."

"Six thousand!" Sergei's mother seemed stunned. "So many?"

"Bianca's shop is one of the best in Texas," Vivian interjected. "Her mother built the business, and Bianca took over when she had a stroke."

"Your mother is better now?"

I nodded. "Yes. She's doing very well."

"This is good."

"You know," Vivian added deftly, "Bianca designed my wedding dress. She also designed Erin's. You'll meet her tomorrow. She's Ivan's wife." Vivian retrieved her cell phone from her pocket and started to swipe through photos. "See? This is Erin's wedding to Ivan. She was a beautiful bride, wasn't she?"

"Very," Galina agreed.

Vivian smiled. "The dress was perfect, all lace and fluttery and feminine."

Galina turned to me. "You went to school for this?"

"I did. In New York."

"I like this..." Galina seemed to be thinking of a word she couldn't find. She spoke a phrase to Vivian who promptly answered, "Silhouette."

"Yes, I like this silhouette." She took the phone from Vivian and held it closer for me to inspect. "Do you design many like this?"

"Maybe a third of my designs are sheaths. They look good on everyone, and they're lighter and more comfortable for those hot summer weddings in Texas. I'm doing more mermaids this year." I made the shape of the skirt with my hands. "They're very popular, especially with beading and lace."

Galina made an agreeing sound. "Yes, but difficult for girls with hips." She drew a heavy hourglass in the air. I didn't miss the way her gaze drifted to my own thick waist and bottom. "Pleats and tucking, this helps."

"Oh, I have quite a bit of experience with hiding curves behind ruching," I said with a laugh. "I mastered that trick in high school."

She smiled at me before glancing back at the phone. Vivian had taken it back and had pulled up photos from her own wedding. Galina studied them. She murmured sweetly to Vivian, no doubt praising her beauty. Eventually, she turned to me with a genuine expression and complimented my work. "You are very talented, Bianca."

Across the table, Sergei winked at me. We shared a tender, private smile. It filled me with hope. She might learn to like me yet.

Dinner ended on a happy note, and I walked downstairs to the lobby to see Vivian into the private car Yuri sent round for her. The journey back to our suite took longer than I had expected. The elevators were packed and busy, but I was in no hurry so I let others cram into the cars and waited. After eating a heavy meal, my stomach wasn't feeling very good, and I worried that the heat and swirling scents of other people would upset my belly. It was safer for everyone if I held back until the crowd thinned.

Eventually, I stepped into a car and hit the button for my floor. The ride was quick. When I reached the door of our suite, I heard the raised voices. With my card poised at the lock, I held my breath and listened carefully. I couldn't understand a word that was spoken, but I easily picked out Sergei's voice and his mother's. They were arguing about something.

About me. It had to be me. There was no other reason for it.

Backing away from the door, I took three steps, whirled around—and slammed into Ivan's chest. Ice cubes rattled in the container he held and spilled onto the carpet beneath our feet.

"Hey!" he said softly and steadied me with one big hand. "Are you all right?"

"I'm fine."

"Are you sure?" He kicked aside the ice cubes so I wouldn't trip over them. "You knocked into me pretty hard." His gaze dropped to my stomach.

Did he know about the baby? "I really am okay."

Behind me, the irritated voices grew louder. Ivan's expression turned dark. He put a hand at the small of my back and urged me forward. "Come. I'm sure Erin would like some company while she watches that fashion reality show she loves so much."

Not at all surprised by his kindness or his urge to protect and shield me, I let him lead me away from the scene in the suite that I simply couldn't stomach to hear.

And yet...

I had to know.

"Ivan?"

He glanced down at me. "Don't ask, sweetheart."

"I am asking. I want to know."

He didn't answer until we had passed two more doors. "It's not you, Bianca. It's old ideas. She likes you."

"But?"

"But she doesn't want him to marry you." He hesitated again, and I could hear his teeth grinding together. "It would be embarrassing for her to explain to their friends."

The air rushed from my lungs. Pain clutched at my heart.

Ivan's hand slipped from the small of my back to my hip. He gave it a gentle, friendly squeeze. "Don't let this upset you. Not now. Not when..." He looked at my stomach again. "It doesn't matter to Sergei. You understand? He loves you. This is all that matters now."

"I know he loves me, but I also know that family means so much to him. How do I ask him to choose between us?"

"You don't." Ivan pressed me forward toward the suite he shared with Erin. "He can have both of you. It won't be easy for him, but things worth having rarely are."

We reached his suite, and he fished the key out of the pocket of his chinos. He opened the door and led me inside. "Erin, look what I've brought you."

She grinned up at me from the sofa where she was curled up in her pajamas. "Bianca! Come sit." She patted the space beside her. "You can help me make fun of these awful skirts they designed."

Kicking off my shoes, I joined her. Sure enough, there were some truly ratchet skirts hanging off the models who moved down the catwalk. Ivan brought Erin a glass of pink champagne, her favorite as I well knew, but he brought me a cup of hot tea. He took the corner spot near Erin and sipped at the champagne his wife preferred. Like a rabbit, he wiggled his nose as the bubbly bite saturated his mouth. I almost laughed at the sight of big, scary Ivan drinking pink champagne.

The show was nearly over when there was a loud knock at the door. By then, Erin was two flutes down but Ivan had long set aside his first one. He answered the door, and I stiffened at the sound of Sergei's voice. He trailed Ivan into the suite and shot me a look of utter consternation. "You didn't come back. I was worried."

"Sorry. I ran into Ivan, and he invited me over to visit with Erin."

"Would you like a drink?" Erin gestured to the bar. "I promised Ivan an action movie after my show. You're welcome to join us."

"No, thank you. My family is waiting."

"Oh! Right." Erin glanced at me with confusion. Whatever she saw on my face made her frown slightly. Tomorrow she would no doubt get the truth out of me.

Setting aside my cup of tea, I rose from the sofa and slipped back into my shoes. "Did Vivian text you?"

"About Thursday?" She nodded. "It sounds like fun. Will your—er—Sergei's mom be joining us?"

"No," I said softly, certain hell was sure to freeze over before she agreed to be seen with me in public.

"Oh. Well..."

I gave a little shake of my head. "I'm going out tomorrow. Give me a call if you want to go."

"Sure."

I patted Ivan's arm as I walked by him. "Good night."

"Good night, Bianca."

Sergei grasped my hand, his fingers warm and soothing around mine. When we were out in the hallway alone, he gently pressed me up against the wall. He boxed me in with his huge body, planting his hands on either side of my head, and peered intently into my eyes. For a long moment, we said nothing. When he spoke, it was with passion. "I love you, Bianca."

I put my hands on his chest and rose on tiptoes to press my lips to his. "I love you, too."

He caressed my face. "Whatever you heard, it means nothing. She'll come around eventually."

I swallowed nervously. "Did you tell her about the baby?"

His jaw visibly clenched. "I did."

"And?" I could scarcely squeak out the word.

"She congratulated us."

I found that hard to believe. "But?"

"But nothing, Bianca. She's happy for us. She's happy about the baby."

He was lying to me, but I couldn't be angry with him. I knew why he was doing it. In a way, I loved him all the more for trying to spare my feelings.

"Let's go to bed. It's been a long day. I'm sure you're tired."

"I am."

He gathered me close and led me back to our room. My heartbeat thundered as we entered our suite but slowed when I realized the main living space was empty. Not wanting to have a weird run-in after that blowup between mother and son, I didn't linger in the living room. Once inside our bedroom, I made quick work of removing my makeup, brushing my teeth and slipping into a nightgown. Sergei joined me not long after and slid into bed behind me.

Not surprisingly, he curled up against my back and pressed loving, tender kisses along my neck and cheek. He embraced me with his strong arms and ran his hands along my curves. Though I enjoyed the heat of his touch and felt the first stirrings of need deep within my core, I knew I wouldn't be able to relax with his family across the hotel suite. Thinking of the fight he had had with his mother cooled my ardor.

Reaching back to pat his hip, I whispered, "Not tonight."

"Not tonight."

Sergei froze with shock. It was the first time Bianca had ever denied him. He wasn't angry or upset, but it stunned him. He tried to convince himself it was fatigue from her pregnancy, but he knew better. He suspected Ivan had overheard his argument with his mother and told Bianca some of it. Ivan wouldn't have told her the worst parts. He was too gentle with women to make her cry or upset her, but he would have been truthful with Bianca.

"I'm sorry." Her voice was faint and small in the darkness of their room.

Holding her closer, he nuzzled his nose to her neck and bit down gently on the spot there that made her moan. His teeth raked the sensitive patch before sucking it hard. She shivered in his arms and made a pleasured sighing sound. He brushed his tongue over the spot he had teased and kissed the shell of her ear. "Don't ever apologize for saying no. I shouldn't be so demanding of you, especially not now."

"I like it when you're demanding," she admitted. "I like knowing that you want me."

"I do want you. All the time," he added with a quiet chuckle. "Just thinking about your soft mouth or this perfect ass of yours," he squeezed her plump bottom, "makes me hard." He peppered noisy kisses on her cheek. "But I'm not a caveman. I can wait."

She rolled over in his arms and burrowed her face between his neck and shoulder. Clinging to him as if she feared he might disappear, Bianca ran her fingers through his hair. Inside he was all twisted up with frustration and disappointment. Not with Bianca. *Never* with Bianca. In this mess, she was totally innocent.

Stroking her back and hair, he held her as she drifted off to sleep. Breaking the news to his mother that he planned to marry Bianca and marry her very soon had gone about as well as he had expected. She liked Bianca and respected her as a businesswoman and a designer. He suspected his mother was more grateful than words could even describe for the way Bianca had saved and freed him.

But the taboo of crossing *that* line to marry her wasn't one his mother could accept so easily. In time, she would come to love Bianca as much as he did. Of that, Sergei was certain. Until then? He had to keep the peace between the two women in his life who meant everything to him.

Because on that account he had been very clear with his mother. He would not allow her to disrespect Bianca or show her unkindness. After everything she had done for him and the love she had gifted him, Bianca deserved to be treated like a queen. His hand moved from her hip to her belly. Soon it would be round and heavy with his baby. No one would be allowed to upset her. No one.

Eyes closed, Sergei blew out a noisy breath and hugged Bianca tighter. Not wanting to think about the ugly fight, he thought about the pretty little girls he had seen running around the hotel lobby. In his mind, he conjured up a child who was everything he loved in Bianca and liked in himself. The image he created soothed the irritation that gripped his gut. That smiling face was worth all of this trouble.

6 CHAPTER SIX

"You look amazing," Sergei breathed with awe when I stepped out of our bedroom on Friday evening.

I had chosen a cocktail dress in the deepest sapphire shade of blue. The design had a slight wraparound effect with a tucked pleat that sat on my left hip. It accentuated the curve of my waist while nipping in my big hips. Unable to stand my usual body shapers right now, I was glad for the structure of the dress and the no-cling fabric that glided over my lingerie.

Sergei hated the spandex and Lycra body shapers anyway. He always growled when he discovered them under my clothing. To him, they were sheer blasphemy. Given the chance, he probably would have tossed them all into the trash. He just didn't understand that sometimes a girl needed some full-coverage support.

"Thank you." I held up the necklace I wanted to wear. "Can you help me?"

He took the necklace and stepped behind me. I had styled my hair up tonight so he had plenty of space to work. His fingers were surprisingly agile despite their size, and he fastened the clasp easily. Never one to pass up the chance to tease, Sergei dropped ticklish kisses on the exposed line of my shoulders and throat. He inhaled slowly and let loose a low groan. "You smell fucking good tonight."

Before I could respond, I noticed movement out of the corner of my eye. Galina had entered the living area just in time to see her son nuzzling up against me. I held my breath and waited for a look of censure, but it never came. She smiled at us, and it seemed genuine enough. Despite that argument her first night in London, she had been kind toward me. She was trying to accept me, so I offered her the same courtesy. Earlier that day we had lunched with Yuri and Lena. It had gone well. We weren't best friends, but with time, anything was possible.

SERGEI II

Sergei pressed a lingering kiss to my temple before crossing the room to speak with his mother. I gathered up the items I wanted for my clutch and slipped them inside. Vladimir found me getting a bottle of water at the minibar. He took the bottle from me and cracked open the top before handing it back to me.

"Thanks, Vladimir." I sipped the cold liquid and hoped it would settle my stomach.

"Vova," he corrected. "We're friends, yes?"

"Yes." I grinned up at Sergei's younger brother. With his wicked sense of humor and deep belly laugh, he reminded me of my brother Perry. It hadn't taken us long to become friends.

"Here." He handed me a small pack of gum. "I found this when I went out to buy black socks. It will help."

I stared at the ginger gum and felt utterly touched that he thought about me. "*Spasibo,* Vova."

He laughed and playfully tapped my cheek. "We'll have you speaking Russian in no time."

"I don't know about that. I'm pretty terrible at it."

"You'll learn. You have a whole lifetime ahead of you."

In that moment, I felt truly welcomed and accepted by him. A whole lifetime with Sergei? I couldn't imagine anything better.

We took two cabs to the art gallery. By the time we arrived, the show was kicking off and soon in full swing. We slipped in and out of the milling crowd and took our time moving around the perimeter of the elegantly lit space to enjoy Vivian's paintings. It was easy to see that Vladimir and Sergei didn't particularly understand the message in her art, but they enjoyed it all the same.

Galina, on the other hand, seemed deeply moved by some of the pieces. The ones that were more sobering and haunting held her attention the longest. We ended up standing shoulder to shoulder in front of one particular mixed media painting. A woman hesitated at an intersection of streets. A three-dimensional effect made it seem as though one street headed down into a shadowy abyss while the other continued straight ahead. The buildings on the straight and narrow street were reflected upside down in the underground path— the underworld.

The message wasn't lost on me or Galina. Sergei's mother exhaled slowly. "She has much to say."

"Yes, she does." Glancing around the room, I found Nikolai and Vivian chatting with Niels and a couple I didn't recognize. Thrilled and relieved that her husband had finally arrived in London, I studied husband and wife. Nikolai's arm curved protectively around her waist. For the first time in weeks, Vivian smiled with genuine happiness. The gorgeous sunburst jewelry glittered under the bright lights of the gallery. Whatever was going on in the background of their lives, the couple seemed to have set it aside.

"Who is that man?" Sergei's gruff voice rasped in my ear. Dipping down to whisper, he shared his body heat with me and surreptitiously gestured toward a far corner of the gallery.

My gaze traveled to the spot he had indicated. My eyes widened with surprise as I discovered Erin talking to a familiar but wholly unexpected face. "That's Teague."

"Teague?"

"Jackson Teague. He's a big time international business lawyer. He works at one of those high-class firms in downtown Houston. He went to school with my brother. They played baseball together. Actually, I'm pretty sure Teague dated Erin for about a year when they overlapped at Rice together."

Sergei stiffened, and I knew what he was thinking. We both tensed up as Ivan weaved his way through the crowd to join his wife and the handsome lawyer. Erin wasn't the least bit interested in Teague, but I could read the attorney's intentions clearly, even from this distance. The look of contempt when Ivan arrived at Erin's side couldn't be missed. When Teague didn't take the hand Ivan offered, I started to worry. When the lawyer dared to kiss Erin's cheek and slip her his card, I expected the worst. *Oh, dear.*

When Sergei made a move to intervene, I touched his arm. "No. Ivan won't make a scene. See? Erin is handling it."

Once Teague was out of sight, Erin tore the card into four pieces and stuffed it inside her full champagne flute. Her hand gently stroked the back of Ivan's neck. He visibly relaxed. Their foreheads touched together, and she whispered lovingly to him. For all his confidence and skill as a fighter, it was clear Ivan still harbored doubts about his ability to make her happy. He loved her so much, and she absolutely lived for him. A childhood filled with neglect and pain hadn't made it easy for the big fighter to trust or believe in himself.

Certain that all was well there, I grasped Sergei's hand and tugged him along to the next painting. We ran into Yuri along the way and spoke briefly with him. Lena was in full PR mode tonight. In a no-nonsense but vampy black dress and gold jewelry, she maintained control over the event, skillfully guiding the journalists and intercepting the ones she deemed troublesome. I didn't know how she managed to move so quickly and gracefully in those sky-high heels.

Lena's gaze narrowed as a blonde woman approached Vivian. Something about the woman seemed to set off Lena's internal radar. She slipped in front of the woman before she could reach Vivian and Nikolai, who had their backs turned as they talked to Sergei's mother and brother. I watched with amusement and a tinge of awe as Lena arched one winged brow and shook her head. She stepped into the woman's personal space. Whatever she said hit its mark. Red-faced and lips pursed, the woman spun on her heel and left the gallery.

When I glanced at Sergei to ask him if he recognized her, I saw the glint of panic in his eyes. "Who is she?"

Sergei put his hand between my shoulder blades and guided me to the next painting. "She's not important."

"Sergei." I stopped walking and stared up at him. "Who. Is. She."

He ran his tongue around the inside of his lower lip. Reluctantly, he answered me. "She's the woman that Nikolai was expected to marry."

My stomach dropped. "What?"

"He never... It was long before Vivian ever came to work at Samovar and things started to get interesting between them. Nikolai never loved that woman, and she couldn't stand him. It was all arranged between her father and the big boss out of Moscow. She came to Houston for graduate school. They were supposed to get close..."

"But?"

Sergei slid his arms around my shoulders and helped me around another couple. "But she fell in love with someone else and Nikolai helped her escape."

"Escape? Where?"

"Houston and her father," he said. "I don't know where. I didn't even know she was back."

"Do you think Lena knows? Because she just tossed her out on her backside."

"I'm sure she knows."

"Yuri?"

"Probably." Shaking his head, Sergei breathed deeply. "But no more of that. I want to talk about us."

"Us?"

"Yes." He reached into the pocket inside his suit jacket and retrieved a key that he used to unlock a door hidden behind a column and potted plants. Surprised, I nevertheless followed him inside the back room of the gallery. He led me through another door that opened into a small stairwell that took us to the roof.

"What's up here?"

"It was hot inside. I thought you might like to get some air, and the view is beautiful."

It was an entirely innocent explanation, but I wondered if that was all this was. He held my elbow and gently guided me across the terrace. The gallery must have hosted functions up here because the space was completely decked out with outdoor furniture and twinkling lights strung up to illuminate the seating areas.

He was right. The view of the city was gorgeous from up here. It wasn't my first trip to London. I had come as a teenager with Mama and Perry. Back then, we had done all the touristy things that Americans were expected to do. This time, I had tried to find new and interesting places to visit with Sergei. This rooftop definitely fit that bill.

Sergei placed his hand on my upper back and rubbed a slow circle. Standing behind me, he shared all that wicked body heat with me. The scent of his aftershave and cologne filled the air. My body thrummed with delight because I knew I would wake tomorrow morning with that smell clinging to my skin.

"I've never been happier than I am with you."

I smiled and reached back to pat the hand he had settled on my shoulder. "I feel the same way."

"I'll do anything to make you happy, Bianca. Anything you want, I'll find a way to make it yours."

Turning slowly, I wrapped my arms around his trim waist and gazed up at him, hoping he could see the depth of my love reflected in my eyes. "I don't need anything else but you."

He lifted his left hand. "Not even this?"

I blinked twice. Was that... I glanced up at him and saw the hope radiating in his expression. My gaze returned to the gorgeous engagement ring sitting on his pinky finger. The brilliant round diamond glittered in a halo setting that included dozens of smaller, equally as perfect diamonds. The platinum glinted under the twinkling lights.

"Sergei!"

"This is all backwards, I know." He sounded apologetic. "I was supposed to ask you to marry me before we made a baby, but I need you to know that I would have asked even if we weren't about to become parents. It's you I want, Bianca. It was you from the first time I saw you with Vivian." He cupped my face in his hands. "You gave me back my life, Bianca. You made me a free man. Share my life with me? Walk beside me from here until the end?"

A sob escaped my throat. His eloquent, heartfelt proposal was exactly what I would expect from him. He understood how to break through my walls and reach me in a way no one else ever could. In just a few sentences, he had reassured me that he wasn't asking me to be his wife out of obligation. He was asking because he loved me and wanted to build a life with me.

"Yes." I placed my hands over his. "I want to share my life with you."

Grinning, Sergei gently clasped my left hand and slid the engagement ring into place. As it glided effortlessly onto my finger, I got a closer look and instantly recognized the craftsmanship and design elements as Zoya's. The jewelry designer and gemologist had a certain flare when it came to her work that was unmistakable.

Sergei lifted my hand and kissed my engagement ring. With a teasing smirk on his handsome face, he said, "I promise I'll never stop kicking down doors for you."

"Not many women can say they fell in love with their future husband when he kicked down a door to save her from a shower curtain," I replied with a laugh.

"I'd do it again." He lowered his face and finally kissed me. "And again." He pecked my left cheek. "And again." His lips touched the right side of my face. "There's nothing I won't save you from, Bianca."

He meant every word he said. A shower curtain, crazy racist thugs—there was nothing that he wouldn't do to keep me safe.

"I love you, Sergei."

He embraced me with his powerful arms. "I love you, Bianca. Always." He kissed the top of my head. "Forever."

Our mouths met in a passionate explosion. Sergei walked backward toward the closest sofa and sank down onto it. He dragged me onto his lap, gripping my bottom and forcing me to straddle him. My skirt was too tight so he shoved it up around my hips and bared my lacy panties to the night air. I gasped against his mouth. "Sergei! We can't."

"Why not?" He was already tugging my undies down my hips. "We're outside. It's dark. The door is locked. No one will find us."

"But—oh!" I moaned as his fingertip dipped into my cleft. "What if someone in another building sees us?"

"Then they see us," he replied calmly.

"Sergei..."

He silenced my protest with a kiss that left me dizzy and clutching at him. Heat pooled between my thighs, and my breasts ached to be stroked and fondled by him. I accepted that I was about to add a new experience to my list that I had never expected to indulge.

"Watch my hair," I begged in between kisses. "Everyone will know what we've been up to on the roof if I come down with my hair a mess."

"I'll try."

Limited because of our restricted clothing, Sergei shifted out from under me and dragged me over to the chaise end of the sectional. He pulled me up onto my knees and ran his hand over my plump bottom. His fingers moved to my pussy, and he probed me gently. Already I was dripping for him. Moaning, I pushed back against his fingers. "Sergei. *Now.*"

My breathless request made him groan. He quickly lowered his zipper and freed his erection. He traced my folds with the tip of his cock and gently caressed my back. "I swear I'll love you sweeter than this when we get back to the hotel. I'll make love to you until sunrise if that's what you want."

And then he was inside me. Sheathed with one rough thrust, he impaled me on that extraordinary shaft of his. Thick and long, it filled me up and reminded me of what a man he was. Even in this position, Sergei found a way to make our coupling tender. He leaned over me and pressed loving kisses to my neck and cheek.

I gripped the arm of the couch and rocked on my knees, meeting his thrusts and encouraging him with my sighs and moans. Sergei grasped my wrist and moved my hand between my legs. When I touched myself, I knew it wouldn't be long. I was right on the edge of climaxing. Squeezing my inner walls, I earned a growl of appreciation from Sergei.

"I can't," he panted with a sense of urgency. "God. *God.*"

For the first time ever, he came first, his blazing hot seed flooding me as he shuddered and jerked. Knowing that I had overwhelmed him made me smile. Closing my eyes, I rubbed my clit a little faster and concentrated on the sensation of Sergei's shaft buried deep inside me. "Oh. Oh. *Ohhh.*"

He gripped my hips and ground against me as I climaxed. Shaking and limp, we fell forward onto the cushions of the sofa. We couldn't stay that way forever. There was a party downstairs, and we would soon be missed.

But as Sergei interlaced our fingers, I blinked away tears while staring at the beautiful ring he had given me. Suddenly I couldn't think of a single reason why we needed to hurry back to the real world.

7 CHAPTER SEVEN

Sitting in bed on Saturday evening, I sketched some wedding dress ideas on the pad I carried everywhere. My pencil glided over the paper. Left handed, I kept stopping to admire the engagement ring glittering on my finger. The memories of last night left me giddy. I held up my hand to study the twinkling diamonds.

Grinning like a fool, I returned to the sketches. I had a bodice in mind for my gown, but it was the skirt that gave me fits. I didn't know when we were going to tie the knot. If it was too far into my second trimester, my options were going to be severely limited.

No amount of corseting, pleats, tucks or ruched organza could hide the big baby belly I would have by then.

"Bianca?" Galina ducked her head through the open doorway. "Would you like dinner?"

Sergei and Vladimir had gone out for a night of pub crawling. I hadn't been thrilled by the idea of spending an evening alone with my future mother-in-law. The feeling seemed mutual. She had disappeared into her bedroom the moment her sons were gone. Not wanting to push myself on her, I had sought refuge in here to sketch and think.

Now she was making an effort, and I understood how hard that was for her. I smiled at her and set aside my sketchpad. "I'd like that. The restaurant downstairs is supposed to be very nice. Would you like to try it?"

"Yes. That sounds good." She came into the bedroom and gestured toward my sketchpad. "May I?"

"Of course." I handed it to her. "Let me duck into the bathroom and change out of these yoga pants and into something a little nicer."

She waved her hand. "Please. I'm happy to wait."

I stood slowly, but a wave of nausea and dizziness still swamped me. Annoyed by the morning sickness, I carefully made my way to the bathroom and closed the door. I had been feeling some twinges along my sides and in my back all afternoon and evening. After losing my lunch and the tea and cookies I had tried to have a few hours later, I figured the aches were from over-exercised muscles. Not even ginger gum and candy were keeping the sickness at bay now.

As I picked out a dress, I realized I had to pee again. I couldn't believe how much time I was spending in the lady's room these days. If I wasn't sick, I had a throbbing bladder. I shuddered to think what it would be like when I was nine months pregnant and this baby of ours was jumping up and down in there. I would have to move my office into one of the stalls at work if I was going to get anything accomplished.

When I sat down, I glanced at my undies and gasped. Bright red blood marred the pale blue cotton. Stunned and horrified, I reached for some toilet tissue and hastily checked to see if I was still bleeding. The evidence made my heart race. "No! No! No!"

Hastily cleaning up, I grabbed a clean pair of panties and found a liner in my toiletry case. My hands were shaking, and my stomach lurched painfully as I tried not to imagine the worst. But that blood! All of that blood.

"Bianca?" Galina knocked on the door. "Are you okay?"

I wanted Sergei. I *needed* Sergei, but he wasn't here. His mother, the woman who had begged him not to marry me, was the only available to help me. The irony of that didn't escape me, even in my panicked state.

"Bianca?" She knocked louder. "What is wrong?"

Trembling and on the verge of tears, I opened the door. Galina's brow was furrowed with concern. She touched my arm, and I sobbed pitifully, "I'm bleeding."

Shock slackened her face. A second later, she schooled her features and grasped my hand. "It's okay. Lots of women bleed. We go to hospital. Everything will be all right. Yes?"

I weakly shook my head, but I didn't believe her. That much blood could only mean one thing. My hand drifted to my belly and fresh tears dripped down my face.

"Sh," Galina embraced me and rubbed my back. "The baby is fine. You see."

As if I were a child, she took my hand and guided me around the hotel room, gathering up my purse and then hers. We left the suite and made our way to the elevators.

Once inside, she squeezed my hand. "When I was pregnant with Vovachka, I bleed every day for three weeks. He was healthy baby. *Big* baby," she added with a reassuring smile. "Just like Sergei."

I clung to her hand and her words. *Please, please, let my baby be okay.*

Everything became a blur after that. Like a mother bear, Galina took charge. She had the hotel's valet hail us one of the waiting cabs and gave him directions to take us to the closest emergency room. She even made sure that I remembered to fasten my seatbelt. In my dazed state, I hadn't even noticed that I had forgotten.

Soon, we were in the waiting room of the hospital. My hand shook as I filled out the forms. I wanted to scream as the minutes ticked by on the clock mounted on the wall across from us. Why weren't they calling me back? Why was this taking so long? *My baby! God, my baby...*

Finally, a nurse called my name. I gripped Galina's hand. "Come with me?"

She touched my cheek. "Let them try to stop me."

"So what are you going to do about the construction company and the offer to work at the gym?" Vladimir drained the last of his beer and dragged his bottom lip down the upper one to gather up the foam clinging to his skin.

Twirling a thin coaster on the pub tabletop, Sergei answered his brother honestly. "I like working with

Ivan, but the boss was right. I have to think long-term, especially now with the baby. I talked to Ivan about it, and he understood my concerns. I'm at the gym to train every morning anyway, so I'm partnering up with the fighters on the underground circuit to get them into shape. He's also asked me to go into the sparring rotation with some of his legitimate fighters. I might not have any official championship belts but I know things you can't learn in a sanctioned match."

"So part-time at the gym and full-time in construction?" Vladimir made a face. "That's a lot of hours, Sergei."

"I've worked harder. The construction company is a lot of office work. It's draining but I'm learning to like it. It's a fucking breeze compared to swinging a hammer." He sipped his beer. "Bianca doesn't want me to pay back the money she spent to buy my contract, but that's a debt I need to wipe clean. Doubling up between the gym and the construction is the fastest way to do that."

Vladimir drummed his fingers on the table. "I've only known her for a few days, but I don't think she'll take the money from you."

"She won't. That's why I'm going to put it into mutual funds for our kids."

"Mutual funds? When did you become an investor?"

"I listened and watched. The boss learned from Yuri and I learned from the boss. Twenty thousand invested now and grown slowly is better than some flashy get-rich-quick scheme. I have to think about my kids' futures. They'll want to go to college and have weddings and buy houses."

His brother grinned. "Kids? You're already planning to have more?"

"We made this one without even trying." He laughed as a surge of masculine pride rocked him. "I have a feeling that five-bedroom house of Bianca's might need an addition before we're done."

Vladimir laughed and shook his head. "I can't believe you're going to be a father. I'm going to be an uncle again."

They both sobered at the memories of the sweet little nieces they had lost. Their older brother's stupidity had taken so much from the family. It was good to have something to celebrate.

"So...the wedding?"

Sergei's mouth twitched with sadness. "I wish you could be there."

"Maybe we can," Vladimir replied hopefully. "We'll try to get travel visas. It might not be possible because we're in the middle of immigration proceedings, but it can't hurt to ask for them."

Sergei started to question Vladimir about his job prospects with Dimitri Stepanov's private security firm when his brother frowned and lifted out of his seat to retrieve his cell phone from his jeans. He glanced at the screen before answering. "Ma?"

The tense expression on his brother's face didn't bode well. Sitting forward, Sergei dropped the coaster and waited for Vladimir to say something.

Vovchik slipped his phone into his pocket and tugged his wallet free. A handful of bills landed on the table. "We have to go."

"Why?" Sergei's chest tightened. "What's wrong?"

Vladimir's serious face scared him. "Bianca is in the hospital." He paused. "It's the baby."

No. He silently repeated the word again and again as they rushed out of the pub and into the night to find a cab. His brother made sure the cab driver knew which hospital they needed before they climbed into the back seat. Hands clammy and stomach knotted, Sergei had never felt so nervous or sick in his life. He hadn't been this panicked even before that first cage match, back when he still feared pain and blood. Now, so many years and opponents later, he didn't even bat an eye at either. The burst of pain and the coppery flash of blood on his tongue was nothing to him.

With his heart thundering in his throat, Sergei jumped out the cab before it had even fully stopped.

Vladimir stayed behind to settle the tab, but was hot on his heels a moment later. Their evening of carousing and good beer seemed like a distant memory. All he could think about now was Bianca and the baby. His stomach twisted painfully.

I should have been there. Why the hell wasn't I with her? If the worst happened tonight, would Bianca forgive him for not being with her? Would he be able to forgive himself? When she had needed him most, he was tossing back a beer and playing darts with his brother. She had urged him to go out and enjoy his last night with Vovchik, but she couldn't have known this was going to happen.

The wait at the reception desk nearly killed him. Only Vladimir's steadying hand on his shoulder kept Sergei from blowing up and demanding somebody speak to him. Finally, a rushed and very busy nurse was able to help him. He tried to remember that she was trying to do her job in a packed unit on a Saturday night.

When he tugged aside the curtain shielding Bianca from the rest of the emergency room cubicles, he stopped dead in his tracks. Rolled on her side, she cried softly while his mother held one of her hands and stroked her hair with the other. The sight of the soon-to-be mother-and-daughter-in-law finding support in one another should have warmed him, but tonight it scared him. How bad was it if his mother had shoved aside all of her prejudices to comfort Bianca?

Wordlessly, his mother pressed a gentle kiss to Bianca's forehead before leaving her side. She joined him at the curtain and patted his chest. She slipped away and left them. Refusing to show the weakness that threatened to cripple him, Sergei strode to Bianca's bedside and took the chair his mother had vacated. Bianca needed him to be strong for her and the baby so he swallowed down the lump of emotion clogging his throat. He interlaced their fingers and captured her mouth in a long kiss. His other hand traveled down her side and settled on her belly. He spanned his fingers across her stomach. Terrified of the answer but desperate to know, he asked softly, "Our baby?"

"I don't know." She gulped loudly and blinked. More tears spilled onto her beautiful face. He wiped them away with his thumb. "They're waiting for an obstetrician to come see me." She gripped his fingers so tightly he thought she might break them. "I'm scared."

"I'm here." He kissed her again, his lips lingering on her soft pouty ones. "Whatever happens, I'm here."

A doctor and nurse arrived a short time later with a portable ultrasound machine. He held Bianca's hand while she talked with Dr. Jones and helped her slide down toward the end of the bed when it was time to examine her. Bianca's gaze drifted to the ceiling while a sheet was draped across her bent knees. This was new territory for him. He wasn't sure what he was supposed to do. All he knew for certain was that he wasn't leaving her side.

When the doctor produced the ultrasound wand, Sergei experienced a moment of surprise. He had assumed it was always done on the belly, but apparently that wasn't true. He kept his gaze fixed on Bianca's worried face while the doctor did what he needed to do. She still gripped his hand so tightly her knuckles had gone white.

"Well, well, well," Dr. Jones said, his voice amused. "I have a feeling you two weren't expecting this."

Sergei's attention jumped to the ultrasound monitor. He couldn't make sense of the grainy black and white image. The image shifted a little as the doctor made an adjustment and suddenly Bianca gasped. It wasn't pain or fear that made her inhale so sharply. It was shock.

"Is that...? Are those...?" Wide-eyed, she gaped at the doctor and nurse. "Twins?"

Sergei damned near fell out of the chair. That wasn't possible. Twins? No. They were having one baby. One fat, healthy baby.

Except now that he looked at the monitor, *really* looked at the monitor, he easily spotted the two black sacs in the center of a fuzzy gray and white circle. Inside those dark sacs were two distinct white baby-like shapes.

My babies.

His heart threatened to burst, as feelings unlike any he had ever known exploded within him. When Bianca had shown him the positive test, he had been stunned and flummoxed but also excited. Until now, until he saw his babies with his own two eyes, it hadn't been truly real. Watching the two tiny shapes move around on the screen left him nearly breathless.

"The babies look fine," Dr. Jones commented. "We've got good, strong heartbeats on both." The nurse used the ball-shaped mouse attached to the machine to help the doctor measure the babies. "Baby A is measuring at seven weeks and one day and Baby B is measuring at six weeks and six days. Those are both in line with your last menstrual period. Now let's see..."

Bianca winced as the doctor tried to find the source of her bleeding. Sergei caressed the back of her hand and hoped the doctor would hurry the hell up and stop hurting her.

"There," Dr. Jones said and gestured to a dark spot on the screen. "It looks like you've got a small subchorionic hematoma. It's basically a blood clot between the uterus and the placenta."

"Is it dangerous?" Fear laced Bianca's voice.

"Not usually," the doctor assured her. "This one isn't very big. It will probably resolve on its own. When you get home, your doctor will continue to monitor you until it dissolves completely. Some practices administer blood thinners to speed up the process but I don't see the need in your case."

Sergei finally relaxed. The ball of pain and worry that had been throbbing in his gut eased up some. He stroked her hair and cheek while the doctor gave them instructions. She was to rest, stay well hydrated and avoid any heavy lifting or exercise until she saw her obstetrician. Dr. Jones stared at him as he delivered the last instruction. "She needs complete pelvic rest, so that means no sex."

"Not a problem," Sergei assured the doctor. He would give up sex for the rest of his life if it meant their babies would be all right. In fact, as he helped Bianca dress, he couldn't shake the feeling that this was his fault. A hematoma was a bruise. Had he done this to her?

Shame gripped him as he thought of all the nights and mornings he had made love to her. How many times had he taken her too roughly? Too deeply? He tried to be gentle with her, but when she started to come around his cock and he felt those silky walls of her pussy gripping him, he struggled to hold back those primitive needs. Faster, harder, deeper. If he had shown more control and care, this wouldn't have happened. He cursed his dick and himself for being so weak.

No more. I won't hurt her again.

Fully dressed and waiting for her discharge papers, Bianca traced the images on the ultrasound printouts the nurse had given her. Watching her stare so lovingly and longingly at their babies made his heart swell. She lifted a teary, happy gaze to his face. "Twins, Sergei. Can you believe it?"

"No," he confessed. He rubbed her earlobe between his fingers and smiled down at her. "We're very lucky."

"Very," she agreed. With a shaky inhale, she said, "I thought preparing for one was scary but two? I don't even know where to start."

"We'll figure it out, Bianca. We aren't the first couple to stumble through this. We've got our families to help us and our friends."

"I'm going to have to start pestering Benny for advice. You'll have to ask Dimitri about the best car seats and cribs and—"

He swept in and silenced her with a tender kiss. Knowing her need to plan everything down to the tiniest detail, he murmured, "Later, Bianca. There is plenty of time for that. Tonight you need to rest."

A nurse brought the necessary paperwork and Bianca signed where indicated. With an arm against her back and his hand on her hip, he walked her out of the emergency room and into the waiting area. His mother and Vladimir had been joined by Vivian and Nikolai. All four were tense and clearly displayed their concern on their faces. The sight of Bianca walking toward them seemed to put them all at ease.

Vivian was on her feet first and hugged Bianca. "I called your phone, and Sergei's mom answered. She told me what had happened. We got here as fast as possible."

Even if Vivian was hurt that Bianca hadn't let her in on their secret, she didn't show it. He suspected Vivian felt guilty for keeping her secret from them. Pulling back, she kept her hands on Bianca's shoulders. "Are you okay?"

Nodding, Bianca made sure to speak loud enough for the others to hear. "It's a blood clot. It's probably not dangerous to the babies, but I have to be careful."

"Babies?" Vladimir seized on the word.

Sergei couldn't stop grinning. "We're having twins."

Now that the fear of a miscarriage had passed, everyone seemed overjoyed for them. Hugs and congratulations were exchanged. To make room for other patients and their families, their small group moved outside. Assured that Bianca and the babies were fine, Vivian and Nikolai said their farewells. Before he got into the idling cab, the boss gripped Sergei's hand. "If you need anything, you call me."

"I will. Thank you."

Smiling, Sergei slapped him on the back. "Congratulations, Sergei. You're going to be a fantastic father."

Certain that was the highest praise he could ever hope to earn from the boss, he stepped back and watched their cab disappear down the busy street. Nestled next to Bianca on the ride back to their hotel, he found himself imagining the wildest things. A vision of his two children playing with Dimitri's daughter and Nikolai's son made him smile. He wasn't sure why he imagined having a son and a daughter with Bianca or why he assumed Nikolai's firstborn would be a son. It felt right.

Back in their suite, he stood outside the shower while Bianca went through her nightly routine and tucked her into bed. He promised he wouldn't be long, but she urged him to take his time and enjoy his family while he could. Out in the living room, he found his mother and Vladimir sitting at the dining table having a late night snack. He joined them.

His mother had the printout from the ultrasound in front of her. She blinked away tears as she gazed at the grainy images of her grandchildren. Whatever her reservations about accepting Bianca into the family, she seemed to be letting them go now. Smiling at her sons, she grasped both of their hands. Sergei refused to think about how very few hours he had left with his mother and brother. Right now they were together. That was all that mattered.

Soon, he promised himself. Soon he would have his entire family—Bianca, their babies, his mother and Vladimir—in the same city. No matter the price, he would make it happen.

CHAPTER EIGHT

Back in Houston, the weeks rushed by so fast. Before I knew it, the last week of August had arrived and with it the end of my first trimester. That bleeding that had scared us so badly while in London had continued off and on through my eleventh week. It had been almost fourteen days since my final day of spotting, and I was finally beginning to believe that frightening episode was over.

My doctor had kept a close eye on me, and sure enough, the clot that was causing me so much grief shrank and shrank until it had disappeared completely. The babies continued to grow on target. Thankfully, my morning sickness had eased up some after hitting its peak around ten weeks. Poor Sergei spent most mornings holding my hair back and dabbing at my neck with a cool washcloth. Sometimes I wondered if he wasn't suffering more than me. He carried so much guilt for my predicament and wouldn't listen when I reminded him we shared that burden equally.

"Bianca, do you need more help?" Vivian tapped at the door to the dressing room I had commandeered at the back of my bridal shop. "Your mama is getting awfully antsy out here."

Connie, one of our bridal consultants, smiled over my shoulder as she finished tightening the corseted back of the gown. She had been with the shop for nine years and knew only too well how difficult Mama could be when she wanted to see a bride in one of her dresses. Renee, the seamstress who had done the final alterations on my gown, helped primp the skirt and snipped away any tiny threads that had been missed.

Staring at my reflection in the mirror, I tried to wrap my head around the image I presented. Organza and satin, pearls and rhinestones—I looked like a freaking princess. A *pregnant* princess, I corrected with a wry smile, but a princess nonetheless.

Between Mama and Galina and a dozen sketches that had gone back and forth via email, we had finally managed to nail down the perfect design. The strapless gown featured a sweetheart neckline and a corseted back that allowed for an easier fit for my baby bump. Ruching paired with dainty pleats and some gorgeous beadwork camouflaged the more pronounced curve to my tummy. The chapel train could be easily bustled for the reception, and the lacy bolero that would cover my shoulders for the ceremony was the perfect compromise.

When I stepped out of the dressing room, Mama gasped and Vivian happily clapped her hands together. Erin bounced up and down in her seat as she hugged the thick binder that she used to organize all the wedding details. Because the store was about to close, most of the staff was free to stand nearby and watch. Some of them clapped. Others grinned and gave thumbs-up signals. Even Ten who hovered in the background while keeping an eye on Vivian showed his approval with the tiniest lift to the corner of his mouth.

Dabbing at her eyes, my mother smiled at me. "Oh, sugar, look at you."

Standing in front of the mirrors, I couldn't believe the transformation either. Even after working in the field for years and years, I was taken aback by the sight of myself in a wedding dress. It wasn't happening the way I had always imagined. That whole thirteen weeks pregnant with twins thing wasn't quite according to plan, but I didn't dare entertain the what-ifs. I trusted that this was always the way it was supposed to be for me. Too many different lives had intersected and changed for the better for me to think otherwise.

I still hadn't settled on the veil I would be wearing, so Junie from our accessories department brought over the two that I liked best. She slipped the first one, a two-tiered fingertip veil, into place and stepped back so everyone could get a good look. She replaced the fingertip veil with a longer walking length veil in a sheer netting.

"The first one," Mama proclaimed from the best seat in the house.

"Definitely," Vivian agreed.

"Yep," Erin chimed with a nod.

Glancing around the room, I noticed only a handful of dissenting opinions. I had Junie attach the fingertip veil again and admired the way it curved around my shoulders and complemented the gown. It really was the perfect fit.

With my veil and headpiece chosen, Mama had Renee make some final adjustments to the gown. She wanted the hem lifted a tad in the front and shook her head when the bustle wasn't just right. Knowing Mama was this exacting with all the brides she helped dress for their big days, I stayed silent and let her do what she did best. Renee made quick notes on the pad she retrieved from her apron and placed pins in the necessary spots.

My second to last fitting came to an end, and I reluctantly slipped out of my dress. I couldn't believe that I would be wearing that and walking down the aisle in a week. In a whirlwind of busy days, it would all be over.

Back in my normal clothes, I found Vivian, Erin, and Mama discussing the wedding preparations. It had been my mother's idea to schedule our wedding for the same weekend as the Perry family reunion. All of Mama's family would already be in town so it was the most logical time to sneak in a wedding on such a short notice. Between all of our friends and my contacts in the industry, pulling together a wedding in seven weeks hadn't been nearly as difficult as I had expected. It was pricier, but Mama hadn't spared any expense.

"So Benny has everything arranged for the delivery of the cake and desserts," Erin said as I joined them. "Yuri is loaning us his backup DJ for the night. Oh, and Nikolai's catering contact said that he wasn't sure we had ordered enough alcohol for the night so he's sending extra, just in case. Whatever isn't opened, he'll take back the next day."

Oddly enough, I didn't even mind that Erin and Mama had taken control of my wedding day. For the first time in my life, I actually enjoyed letting someone else shoulder the responsibility. I had been doing a lot of reading about pregnancy and had decided that my constant on-the-go lifestyle where I was always rushing to meet a design deadline or spending fourteen hours at the shop had to stop. I refused to put the twins at risk.

By Valentine's Day, I would be on maternity leave. I had already started talking to some of the senior employees about the changes that would occur once the twins were here. Mama and I had shared several long discussions about the best way to move forward with the business. There were already key employees in support positions who were more than qualified and trusted to take over some of the duties I had insisted on piling onto my already overflowing plate. Running a small but thriving business was always going to be hard work, but I had to stop making it even harder on myself.

On the drive to the new house Mama shared with Aunt Penny and Aunt Sara, I chatted with her about the upcoming reunion. There was some big drama over the Saturday barbecue sign-up sheet that had everyone in a tizzy. Some of the older women in our family were so territorial when it came to the potluck dishes. I didn't really understand what was so insulting about Uncle Terry's new wife bringing the potato salad.

Mama clucked her teeth and muttered under her breath. It sounded an awful lot like she had said, "Dirty tart," but I convinced myself I had simply misheard. Upstart. Yeah, that was it. She had called my new Aunt Molly an upstart. Because I simply could not fathom my mother calling someone a tart. I just couldn't go there.

"I had a call from Adam Blake's social worker," Mama announced as I pulled into the driveway of her house. It was a damned good thing I was about to put the car into park because I nearly slammed on the brakes in surprise at hearing his name.

"What?" I twisted in my seat to face her. "What did that monster want?"

"He wanted to see if we would be willing to meet with him. It's part of a face-to-face program that allows inmates and victims to speak openly."

The thought of sitting across from the man who had beaten me and murdered my brother sickened me. "Why? What could he possibly have to say to us?"

"He wants to apologize."

I scoffed. "He can write a letter."

"It's not the same, Bianca." Mama toyed with the strap of her purse. "I said yes."

I could not believe what I was hearing. "What? Without even asking me?"

"I'm asking you now." The corners of her mouth pulled tight. "Do you want to come with me?"

"No, I don't, but you know I will." Irritated that she had boxed me into this position, I shook my head. "When do you plan to have this get-together?"

She shot me a look that warned me to watch the sass. "The social worker discussed early October."

I tried to picture my schedule and didn't see any conflicts. The possibility of Adam bringing up his brother Derek in the conversation bothered me. What my mother didn't know was that Adam's older brother had attacked and attempted to kill me in the storeroom of the shop earlier in the summer. Sergei, Nikolai, and Kostya had arrived in time to save me, but the three men who had come there intending to do me harm that night had never been seen again. I worried that Adam might have more sinister intents than his supposed desire for forgiveness.

"Would you like to come inside for dinner?"

"No, ma'am." Feeling suddenly tired, I sagged against the seat.

"Go home and get to bed, honey. Growing one baby is hard enough but two?" She shook her head. "You need to keep those feet up in the evenings and make sure you're getting in bed early."

"I am, Mama."

"Good. Oh, that reminds me." She reached into her purse and produced an envelope. She tugged the card out of it and handed it to me. "I got this from your mother-in-law yesterday! Vivian helped translate the part at the bottom for me."

Surprised by the contact Galina had made with my mother, I read the short note Vivian had translated. It was really sweet and heartfelt. I hadn't told my mother about the early friction with Sergei's mother. There wasn't anything to be gained from it. Honesty truly was not the best policy in all situations.

"This was very nice of her." Galina was trying, and I respected her for that. I understood this wasn't easy for her, and I felt myself warming more and more toward her as she proved how much she loved Sergei and wanted him to be happy, even if he found that happiness with me.

"I'm going to send a card to her. Vivian offered to help."

That didn't surprise me in the least. After tucking the card back into her purse, Mama leaned over to kiss my cheek. When she reached for the door handle, I asked, "Do you want me to help you?"

She shook her head. "I've got this."

And she did. I couldn't believe how well she was doing these days. She easily slid out of the passenger seat and hauled herself to a standing position. Her balance was so much better, and she walked confidently on her prosthetic. I waved at her when she reached her front door and waited until she was safely inside to back out of the driveway.

When I got home, the house was dark. I switched the security system to the at-home setting, had a cup of yogurt with some raspberries and blueberries mixed in for a quick dinner and trudged upstairs to shower. Tonight was Sergei's late night at the gym when he sparred with one of the fighters Ivan was taking to that big mixed-martial arts tournament in Vegas.

As I swiped a lathered sponge up and down my arms, I suddenly remembered that Sergei would be out of town the first week in October. He was going as Ivan's backup coach for the tournament. I already dreaded telling him about the meet-up Mama wanted to have with Adam Blake. I had a bad feeling he was going to get all alpha-crazy when I told him that he couldn't come as my bodyguard.

Not wanting to go down that road, I let my thoughts take a different turn. Standing under the pounding stream of hot water, I slid my hands over my changing body. Heavier and fuller, my breasts weighed down my hands in a way I hadn't expected. My nipples were so sensitive lately, I had even switched out my usual bras, opting instead for seamless cups and no underwire. Curious, I slid my hands down my ribs to my belly.

While I had always had a curve to my tummy, this new roundness was firmer. I put both hands on my stomach and outlined the bump there. With twins growing inside me, I was showing much earlier than most women would, even with my plus-sized body. Vivian had managed to keep her pregnancy a secret until late July when she and Nikolai had announced their news to all of their friends at a cozy dinner party. Now, halfway through it, she could no longer hide the truth with loose tops or big handbags. On her petite frame, every pound showed so easily.

Running my soapy hands over my belly, I wondered when I would experience quickening. All the books said it was coming soon. With two babies dancing around in there, would it feel stronger? I still marveled at the idea of two tiny lives existing inside me. Some days it felt so surreal I could hardly believe it.

After toweling off and going through my normal moisturizing routine, I slid between the sheets without putting on a stitch of clothing. Naked in our bed, I was insanely aware of Sergei's scent lingering on his pillow and the sheets. Because I had been advised to be careful, we hadn't been intimate since the night he had proposed to me, and it was really starting to wear on my nerves.

I had been cleared for sex two weeks ago, but Sergei still refused to touch me. He seemed convinced that what had happened was his fault. I had tried and tried to explain to him that the hematoma happened during conception, but he wouldn't accept that. For some reason, he seemed determined to punish himself—and me.

Alone in the house and starting to experience those stirrings in the feminine center of me, I let my hand drift down my body. I hadn't needed to bring myself to orgasm since that night Sergei had kicked down my front door. He had always been too happy to help me find release, but if he wasn't going to lend a hand...? Well...I would just have to make do with fantasy.

Eyes closed, I tried to replace the feel of my hands with his, but it wasn't possible. My hands were so much smaller and softer. When Sergei touched me, those long thick fingers of his seared my skin. He had rough fingertips that awoke every nerve ending and left tingling swaths on my body. His big hands squeezed and caressed me like no others ever had or would. He owned me—with his kisses and his touches and the gentle way he whispered my name while fucking me like some feral beast, always harder and faster and rougher than I had ever imagined enjoying.

Lightly pinching my nipples, I remembered the time he had straddled my waist after making me come.

He had slipped his cock between my breasts. His shaft had still been slick and shiny with the wetness of my arousal. He had pressed my breasts together, creating a tight furrow that he thrust his cock between again and again.

The handful of lovers I had had before him had never dared anything so brazen. Sergei didn't let a silly thing like modesty or propriety stop us from having fun. Nothing was taboo to him. He encouraged me to let loose and try new things. As of yet, I hadn't been disappointed.

When I had opened my mouth and let him bump that blunt crown against my lips, he had gone crazy. Thrusting faster and harder, he pressed my breasts together even tighter. I had scratched my nails down his thighs until he shuddered and panted. He had dropped forward then, pressing his cock between my lips to thrust against my tongue. Two snaps of his hips, and he had gifted me with burst after burst of his cum.

I had still been swallowing down his essence and wiping the traces from my lips when he had turned toward my feet and planted his knees next to my shoulders. Shoving my thighs wide apart, he had attacked my pussy from an angle I hadn't expected. I had come so hard I nearly blacked out.

Remembering the way his tongue had moved between my folds, I slid my fingers through my wetness and swirled them around my clitoris. The little nub ached and throbbed. Running my fingers down my slit, I played with my opening but didn't penetrate myself. My fingertips returned to that spot that gave me so much pleasure. Imagining my fingers belonged to my soon-to-be husband, I moaned his name. *"Sergei."*

A rough growl echoed in the stillness of the house.

Gasping, I bolted upright and nearly died from embarrassment. With his wide shoulders filling the doorway of our bedroom, Sergei watched me with heavy-lidded eyes. He ran his hand down the obvious outline of his erection that strained against his jeans. "Don't stop on my account."

Torn between mortification at being caught masturbating and the desperate need to finish, I fell back to my pillow and rubbed my clit. If he wanted a show, I was damned well going to give him one.

9 CHAPTER NINE

Sergei didn't think he had ever seen anything more erotic than Bianca playing with her pussy. Her delicate fingers traveled through the slick folds of her cunt, gliding in the shiny wetness that coated her soft flesh. The scent of her arousal saturated the air and made his cock pulse. Balls aching, he watched her flick her clit.

It occurred to him that he had been uncommonly selfish by denying her what she so obviously needed. Even after her doctor had given them permission to resume their normal bedroom activities, he had held back. An irrational fear that he would hurt their babies had scared him and left him feeling uneasy. Watching her now, he couldn't remember why the hell he had allowed himself to be so easily convinced that making love to her was dangerous.

She needed him. She wanted him. He had sworn to make her happy, hadn't he? He was damned well going to make good on that promise!

Toeing off his sneakers, he kicked them aside and strode toward the bed. He peeled out of his shirt, unzipped his jeans and shoved them down his hips. His boxers followed along with his socks. Bianca kept circling her clit while she watched him strip. Ruddy and throbbing, his cock stood at attention. He would get his satisfaction soon enough, but this was all about her.

Sliding down onto his stomach, he clasped her inner thighs and nuzzled between them. The familiar scent of his woman made his body hum with desire. Wanting a taste of all that pink, he wasted no time teasing her tonight. With the pointed tip of his tongue, he swiped her slit from the opening to the very top and then back down again. She howled and rocked her hips for more.

Happy to indulge, he explored Bianca's pussy with his tongue, driving her wild in the process. Her taste had shifted to something sweeter and thinner. He couldn't get enough. Probing her, he flicked and fluttered his tongue in the ways that made her cry out and thrust her cunt against his mouth. When he suckled her clit, she almost shot off the bed. She came, crying his name again and again, but he wasn't done with her, not even close.

He lapped at her clit, humming against that tiny pearl and swirling his tongue around it. Her breaths deepened, and her voice started to climb that octave that told him she was close again. He let one of his hands ride the curve of her belly to settle on her breast. Palming her supple flesh, he found her nipple and pinched the dark peak until she screamed his name. He smiled triumphantly and licked and licked until she threaded her fingers through his hair, grabbed a handful and tugged him away from her pussy.

"No more," she pleaded. "God, no more."

He wiped his mouth on her inner thigh and nipped at her soft skin. She gasped but didn't pull away from him. He loved when she was like this. On one hand, she was overwhelmed by pleasure and couldn't take any more. On the other, she was still hot and aching. Lucky for her, he knew exactly what she needed.

Sergei kissed his way up her body, dotting his lips against her thighs and lower belly and around the swell of her stomach. He couldn't quite believe she was already a third of the way through the pregnancy. His hand curved protectively over the small bump. Holding her gaze, he promised, "I won't hurt you."

Her expression softened. "I know that."

"I'll be gentle."

Seeming to understand that he was saying these things more to remind himself than her, Bianca sweetly caressed his face. "Make love to me, Sergei. I need you."

He pushed up on to his knees and placed a steadying hand next to her arm. They traded increasingly passionate kisses. Their tongues darted in and out of each other's mouths, flicking and touching and stoking a fire that threatened to burn them both right up. He nibbled her lower lip, and she sucked his.

Thrusting his hips forward, he rubbed the rigid length of his cock against her hot pussy. She groaned and wrapped her legs around his waist. Pressing her heels into his backside, she dragged him closer. "Please, Sergei."

Loving the way she begged for his cock, he took his shaft in hand and guided it down to her sopping wet entrance. Because it had been awhile, he didn't try to bury himself in her on one thrust. He took his time with her, gliding in a few inches and retreating and then sliding back inside even deeper. She clutched at his sides, her beautifully manicured nails digging into him, but he didn't mind. He relished the sting.

Capturing her mouth, he rocked into her. Feeling the curve of her belly between them, he recognized the days of enjoying sex in this position were numbered. He stabbed his tongue between her lips and let his hands roam her body. He couldn't get enough of her lush curves. Gazing into her dark eyes, he lost himself for a moment. Erotic and breathtaking in her beauty, she enthralled him like some mythical creature. In her, he had found his reason for living. She was everything to him—his lover, his friend, the mother of his children.

Home. He chased the buzzing feeling building low in his stomach. *She feels like home.*

After leaving his family and his country in a bid for survival, he had always felt like an outcast. He was part of Nikolai's family, but that wasn't real. It wasn't love. It was blood and pain and violence. What he had with Bianca was the complete opposite. She was the antidote to the poison of the mobbed-up hell he had been forced to live for too long.

"I'm coming," she whispered on a shocked gasp. "Sergei!"

Burying his face against her throat, he plunged in and out of her while her slick pussy gripped and released his cock. He welcomed the shuddery rush deep in his belly. Toes curled, he climaxed with a sound close to a sob. Bianca rubbed the back of his neck and scratched idly at his scalp while he slumped against her, not yet wanting to move away from her womanly softness.

Eventually, he dropped onto his side and curled his arms around her. She snuggled in tight, burrowing into him and seeking the heat he happily shared. Too damned spent to reach down to grab the sheet, he slung a leg over both of hers and pulled her in even closer. She drew shapes on his chest and kissed his skin every now and then

"Sergei?"

"Yes?"

"What happened to the Night Wolves?"

He stiffened at the mention of the racist gang who had tried to kill Bianca earlier in the summer. They had made the mistake of threatening Vivian while they were at it. The boss had answered their threats with violence unlike any that crew had ever known. He had wiped them off the city map, leaving only three of the original gang still standing. Maimed and broken, they had escaped the Feds who had rounded up their friends and now lived as a warning to anyone else who tried to cross Nikolai's family and the ones he protected. Despite no longer being part of the inner circle, Sergei had heard that a larger organization, one not prone to such stupid acts of senseless racist violence, was making inroads. Whether that was true or if they had the boss's blessing to do business in Houston, Sergei didn't know.

Lifting his head, Sergei frowned at her. "Why are you asking about them?"

Bianca nervously tapped her finger against his chest. She avoided his gaze. "Well..."

Worried, he pressed her down onto her back and loomed over her. "Why are you asking about those assholes?"

"Adam Blake contacted Mama. He wants to meet with us."

His jaw dropped. "For *what*?"

"He wants to apologize."

"Apologize?" Sergei laughed harshly. "He killed your brother and beat you bloody, Bianca. There is no apology in the world that makes up for that."

She sat up and frowned at him. "Maybe he's changed. Maybe he really wants forgiveness."

Sergei made a choking noise. "Forgiveness?" He sneered the word. In case she had somehow forgotten, he repeated, "He *killed* your brother. He left you bleeding and broken in the stockroom of a convenience store. He—"

"I was there, Sergei," she snapped angrily. "I remember vividly what happened. You don't need to run down the details for me."

His chest tightened at the pain etched into her face. Touching her arm, he shook his head. "You can't actually believe he means any of this, Bianca."

"What if he does?" She gulped nervously. "When Derek had me tied up in the back of the shop, he told me his brother had changed. He told me that was why he wanted to hurt me. He hated me for making his brother weak."

Guilt and shame tore at Sergei. The memory of how close he had come to losing Bianca burned through him like acid. It was a failure he had sworn never to repeat.

"Mama has already agreed to go. She asked me if I would come with her to meet him, and I said yes."

Shocked that she would be so reckless, he growled, "No."

She scowled at him. "Yes."

"No." He slashed his hand through the air. "This isn't up for debate. You. Are. Not. Going."

"My mother is going so that means I'm going with her. This isn't your decision to make."

"The hell it's not!" He gawked at her. "Tell me you are not this blind, Bianca. Don't you understand how dangerous this is? You will be walking into a fucking prison filled with murderers and rapists—"

"Who are all behind bars," she hotly retorted.

"And that means you'll be safe? Is that it? What about the parking lot? What about the road to the prison? What about the guards? Do you have any idea how fucking easy it is to buy someone?"

"How is any of that different than me spending time with your old friends or with Vivian? Huh? Ten? Ex-con. Ivan? Ex-con. Nikolai? Ex-con."

"That's different!"

"Why?"

"Because they don't want to kill you! They don't want to hurt you. If you go inside that prison, you are totally exposed."

"Why do you always have to focus on the very worst possibility?"

"Have you forgotten what happened to my brother and his family? Have you forgotten what I used to be?" He held up the hands that had hurt so many. "These hands have only touched you with love but they beat other men. They caused pain and destruction. I *know*, Bianca. That's why I focus on the worst possibility."

Staring at his hands, she swallowed. "Ten warned me that what you had done wouldn't wash off."

Sergei vowed then and there to kick that tattooed bastard's ass from one end of Houston to the other. "What else did he say?"

"That we wouldn't get to ride off into the sunset together," she confessed. "That you would never truly be out."

Irritated by the ugly reminder of the reality of their situation, he crossly replied, "You should be glad I'll never free then. Since you're so keen on making lunch dates with prisoners, you need all the favors I can get."

Bianca surprised him by snatching up her pillow and hitting him with it. "Stop being so nasty about this."

Taking the pillow from her, he tossed it aside. "You need to stop being so naïve. This is exactly why I don't like that support group. They've got you all twisted up. They've convinced you that you owe forgiveness to these monsters who stole from your families."

"Stop!" Bianca snarled the word. "You do not get to sit there and talk trash about the support group. You're the one who is all twisted up with rage and anger toward dead people. You hate the criminals who slaughtered your brother and his wife and their daughters, but you know who else you hate? You hate your brother for being stupid and putting your family in that position. You hate him for getting you all tangled up in the mob." She jabbed an angry finger at him. "You're the one who needs to learn some forgiveness."

Sergei clenched his teeth together so hard he expected them to shatter. Flayed by her words, he loathed himself for exposing his weakness to the only person in the entire world who could hurt him. He didn't give two shits what anyone else said to him or about him, but Bianca? Her disappointment and anger cut him right down to his soul.

Sliding off the bed, he reached for his discarded boxers and hopped into them. "You aren't going to this meeting. End of fucking story."

"Wrong." Bianca clambered off the bed. "You don't get to tell me what I can and can't do. I'm not Vivian. You're not going to keep me locked away in a golden cage like Nikolai does."

"Is that what you think?" He snorted derisively. "Do you have any idea what sort of trouble her father has caused down in Mexico? Do you know what those people will do if they get ahold of her? What they will do to the baby? They nearly killed Besian Beciraj a few weeks ago. They put a bullet through his chest— and he's a boss. He's one of the hardest, most dangerous men I have ever met, and they nearly took him out." Shaking his head, he added, "I would have thought the taste Derek Blake gave you would have been enough to help you understand what's at stake."

She tried to hide her fear but he could see it plainly. "This isn't about Vivian and Nikolai. It's about us.

I mean it, Sergei. You don't get to make decisions for me."

"The hell I don't!" Why didn't she understand? Was she being deliberately obtuse? "I am the father of those babies." He pointed at her naked belly. "When I'm your husband, it will be my job to keep you safe. Sometimes that means telling you things that you don't want to hear."

"Yeah? Well. You're not my husband yet. Maybe that's a good thing."

His heart fluttered in his chest. A flash of pain stabbed his gut. Silence stretched between them. The weight of her unspoken threat dropped into his stomach like an anvil. He saw the regret flashing in her eyes, but he didn't know what to think.

Bending down, he grabbed his jeans and tugged them onto his legs. Cold inside and emotionally shredded, he snatched up his shirt and left their—*her*—bedroom. Out in the hallway of a house where he was really only a guest, it hit him suddenly how stupid he had been. From their first kiss, he had committed himself to Bianca wholly and completely and without question. She was the woman he had wanted all his life, and he had given up everything for her.

Numb and dazed, he grabbed his keys and left. He realized he was barefoot when the dewy grass cushioned his soles but he didn't turn back for his shoes. *Fuck it.* He didn't even care.

Once behind the wheel of his SUV, he had no idea where to go. He simply backed out of her driveway, turned down the alley and started driving aimlessly through the streets of Houston. Not so long ago, he would have known every single dark deed about to go down in every dirty corner of the city. He would have known about the heists, the deliveries, the hits and the beatdowns on the underworld calendar. Now he didn't even know if the new white supremacist crew who had taken over the Night Wolf action had unfinished business with Bianca.

There was an easy way to find out. All he had to do was pick up his phone and call the boss, but once that door was reopened? He would never be able to shut it again. He had been allowed to walk away. If he came back and asked a favor like this one? He would be in Nikolai's debt again. Friend or not, the boss would expect to collect someday. He was already tied up in a neat little knot with the construction company, but if he asked for some sort of safe passage for Bianca inside a prison? Jesus. He would really be in deep then.

But what else was he going to do? She was so damned stubborn. She had called his bluff in her bedroom. He could bark all he liked, but now she knew there were no teeth behind his snarls. He wasn't that man. He refused to be that man. He might make a lot of noise, but they both understood he didn't have it in him to crush her spirit and forbid her anything.

Because I'm weak when it comes to her.

It was a painful thing to accept. There was fucking nothing on this planet he could deny her. His stomach lurched as he acknowledged the ugly truth. In the morning, he would go crawling back to her and apologize. He had been overbearing and rude. In his desperate attempt to protect her, he had overstepped the line.

It was nearly three in the morning when he finally returned to her house. The gate slid open silently, and he pulled into his usual spot. When he killed the engine and his eyes adjusted to the darkness, he spotted Bianca sitting on the back steps of the house. His heart raced as worry overwhelmed him. Had she been sitting there all fucking night?

Bailing out of the SUV, he rushed across the backyard. She stood slowly, and he instantly wrapped his arms around her body. "Are you all right?" He could feel the dampness in her clothing. "*Milaya moya.*" He shook his head. "What were you thinking?"

"You left," she stated pitifully. Her voice was husky and raw as if she had been crying for hours. The realization that she probably had been slashed him like a razor.

"I came back." He embraced her tightly. "I'll always come back."

"I'm sorry, Sergei." She sobbed against his chest and fisted his shirt in her hands. "I'm so sorry. I didn't mean it. I love you. Please don't go away."

"I'm not going anywhere." He kissed her temple. "I was angry, and I needed some space to think. Maybe we both did." Thinking of the babies, he urged her inside. "You need to change and get into bed. This isn't healthy."

She clung to his arm while he led her into the house and up to her—*their*—room. He peeled away the damp nightgown and pulled one of the dainty silky things she liked over her head. It hugged the outline of her pregnant belly in the most alluring way. Even so drained after their fight, he still couldn't help his body's response to her.

Shedding his clothes, he dragged her into bed with him and curled around her. She kissed his arm and whispered in the darkness. "I know you only wanted to protect me."

"I shouldn't have been such an asshole about it."

"I shouldn't have threatened to call off the wedding. That was low and dirty." She pressed back against him as if afraid he might disappear. "I didn't mean it, Sergei. I love you, and I want you to be my husband."

"Even if it means we're going to fight like this?"

"Maybe we only fight like this because our love is strong," she reasoned. "If you didn't love me as much, you wouldn't have made such a fuss."

Certain that it was going to piss her off, he nevertheless said, "I still don't want you to go."

"I don't want to go either," she admitted, "but I promised Mama I would go with her." Her voice grew softer and smaller. "I'm afraid that Adam will say something about Derek. He has to know what happened that night. What if he intends to hurt us?"

I'll fucking kill him. There was no doubt in his mind. If Adam Blake so much as joked about hurting Bianca or their babies, he would sneak into that prison and do the job himself. That awful bastard had taken enough from her. He wasn't going to get the chance to hurt her children too.

"He can't hurt us," Sergei said instead. "He's in prison, and he's been crippled. He's isolated on the inside. His crew is either dead or locked up. He has no power."

Though he was sure he would one day regret it, he offered the only thing he could. "If you intend to go, I'll speak to Nikolai. He'll make sure it's safe for you and your mother to go to the prison."

She turned over in his arms. He could feel her eyes boring into him but couldn't see them in the darkness. "What will he want in return?"

"Nothing," he lied, refusing to upset her. "He owes me favors still. I'll call them in to make sure you're safe."

She didn't say anything. Was she doubting him? If she did, she didn't dare mention it. "Sergei?"

He stroked her hair. "Yes?"

"I'm sorry about what I said about your brother. That was so wrong. I shouldn't have gone there."

He swallowed hard, but kept caressing the back of her head. "It was true. You shouldn't apologize for the truth."

"It hurt you."

"Sometimes the truth hurts."

"I love you. I'm not supposed to be the one who hurts you."

You're the only one who can.

"It's all right." He kissed her tenderly. "It's done, Bianca. I've let it go. So should you."

She sought his mouth and sweetly trailed her fingertips down his cheek. Her lingering kiss eased the remaining hurt. He wasn't angry at her. He truly had let it go. In the heat of the moment, they had both said stupid things, but their love and this relationship they were building were too important to hold grudges.

SERGEI II

He waited until he felt Bianca relax in his arms to let sleep take him. It didn't take long for his happy dreams to take an ugly turn. The last thing he remembered before bolting awake were the snarling, dripping fangs of a white wolf sinking its cruel teeth into Bianca's heavily pregnant belly.

Wiping a hand down his sweaty face, he rolled onto his side and buried his face in her fragrant hair. Swearing to keep her safe, he made plans to see Nikolai as soon as possible. There was no deal he wouldn't make to protect her.

10 CHAPTER TEN

"Are you ready?" Vivian smiled as she stepped in front of me to primp my veil.

"Yes." That fight we had had almost a week earlier had been terrible, but it had driven home how very much I loved Sergei and wanted him in my life. There were always going to be arguments, but I felt reassured that we could get through them.

I'll always come back. I remembered his huskily spoken reassurance. Even after I had hurt him so badly, he still came back. *Because he loves me.*

"How are you feeling?" Vivian eyed my belly with worry before pressing a bottle of water into my hand.

"Don't drink too much because you don't want to have to ask for a potty break before your vows."

"I'm feeling good." *Tired*, I added silently. Holding the wedding during our family reunion weekend was smart as far as scheduling went, but it was hard on my pregnant body. Yesterday's barbecue had been so much fun, but it had gone late into the evening. Being on my feet in the September heat had really drained a lot out of me.

"Your family seems to really love Sergei." Vivian took the water bottle from me. She grabbed a tissue and dabbed at my lips before reaching for my chosen lip color to touch up my lipstick. "I heard your cousins making fun of his horseshoe throwing and washer pitching skills."

I laughed as she painted color on my pout. "He was terrible. I mean, you would think that as athletic as he is, there's nothing he can't do. Apparently there is."

"Maybe that's a good thing." She stepped back to admire her work. "He's such an intimidating guy. Seeing him struggle at something makes him human. Plus, he gets that funny look on his face when he's really determined to do something." Vivian mimicked the expression and made me laugh. "See? Even you aren't immune."

She turned to drop the lipstick onto the dressing room counter. "Oh, shoot! We forgot this." Like a drunken bachelor, she whirled my lacy garter above her head. "Skirts up, Bianca. I'm going in."

"You're crazy, you know that?" I gathered up the front of my skirt as carefully as possible to avoid wrinkles and lifted the fabric. Shaking my head, I watched my pregnant best friend duck under my skirt. The sunburst necklace she had received from Nikolai to celebrate her first international show nestled in her cleavage. "Lord help us if anyone comes in here."

She giggled and tapped my right leg. "Lift."

I balanced precariously on one high heel while she slipped the garter into place. Her ticklish touch made me giggle, and she playfully smacked my leg. "Hold still!"

"Stop tickling me!"

"I'm not."

"Yes, you are. I swear you're worse than Sergei."

She snorted in a very unladylike way. "How does that feel? Too low?"

"No, I think it's—"

The door to the dressing room suddenly opened, and I found myself gawking at none other than Sergei's mother. My jaw dropped. "Galina? How did you—?"

But her gaze was fixed on the legs poking out from under my skirt. Right behind her, Mama stepped into the dressing room and gasped with surprise. "Well! My goodness, Bianca!"

Laughing and with hair tousled by my skirt, Vivian slowly backed out and stood. She put a hand on the curve of her back and another on the swell of her belly. "She forgot to put on her garter."

My mother and Galina both looked relieved that nothing truly scandalous had happened. While Vivian rearranged my rumpled skirt, I turned to Sergei's mother. They had been denied the necessary permits in early August, so we hadn't expected to see them again until after the babies were born and we could travel to Europe. "How did you get here? I thought you couldn't get travel visas?"

Galina's grateful gaze fell on Vivian. My friend shrugged and continued to smooth out my skirt. "Nikolai wanted to give Sergei a nice wedding gift."

Even though I was sure less than legal things had happened to make this possible, I chose not to look a gift horse in the mouth. Hauling her close, I hugged her tightly. "Thank you, Vivi."

She rubbed my back and fluffed my veil. "Family is everything. We wanted to make sure all of your family was here with the two of you."

I grasped her hand and gave it a squeeze. There were so many things I wanted to say, but I couldn't find the words to explain to her how much her friendship had meant to me. Maybe she didn't need to hear them. She smiled at me in a way that told me she already knew.

"Bianca," Mama gently interjected, "it's time."

A bit nervous but mostly excited for what awaited me, I hugged Sergei's mother. "*Privet,* Galina."

She touched my cheek and smiled. "You look so beautiful, Bianca. I am happy that Sergei found you."

"Thank you." I hoped she could see how much that meant to me. "I'm so glad he found me, too."

"Here." She opened her hand and surprised me with a bracelet. "I gave this to Sergei when he came to America. Now I give it to you."

I blinked rapidly when I realized she had taken the St. Sergius medallion she had given Sergei for protection and had had it turned into a beautiful bracelet for me. I had noticed that his necklace had gone missing after our return from London. He had played it off and told me that he had probably left it behind. Now I knew the truth. *Sneaky, sneaky!*

She fastened the delicate gold braid around my wrist. "There."

I leaned forward and lightly kissed her cheek, careful not to leave a big lipstick mark. "Thank you."

Her gift given, Galina hugged me one last time and left the dressing room with Vivian. Mama lingered a moment longer. She adjusted my veil and fluffed my skirt twice before threading her arm through mine and leading me out of the room. Without my father or my brother to walk me down the aisle, she was doing the honor for me. I couldn't imagine asking anyone else to do it. She was the woman who had guided and shaped my life.

By now, all of our friends and family knew that I was pregnant. I experienced the smallest quiver of embarrassment as we drew near the doors of the church, but I shoved down that shame. We had broken a rule, but I was never going to be made to feel bad about the twins. They were made out of love, and I intended to make sure they always knew that they were very much wanted and desired.

The doors were flung open, and the processional music began. Our ring bearer and flower girl entered the church first and then Vivian followed not far behind. Instead of a huge wedding party, I had opted for only a matron of honor. Until the surprise arrival of Sergei's mother and brother, Ivan had been tapped to stand as best man, but I had no doubt Vladimir would be standing next to Sergei now.

With my mother at my side, I slowly made my way down the aisle of a packed church. My family and friends had overflowed to the back pews of Sergei's side, but he had a surprising showing, too. I almost did a double-take when I spotted Ten in a suit and tie at the end of one of the front pews. He looked shockingly handsome, but still just as dangerous. Nikolai stood in the first row with Sergei's mother, Ivan and Erin. Yuri and Lena and Dimitri, Benny and Sofia were behind them.

And there, waiting for me at the end of the aisle, was Sergei. Standing proud and tall, he looked devastatingly handsome in his tuxedo. Vladimir stood next to him, a friendly grin making him look so carefree and happy. He actually reached out and clapped Sergei's shoulder. I couldn't hear what he said, but whatever it was, Sergei nodded and smiled.

When Sergei reached for my hand, I placed my fingers atop his. My eyes widened when I felt the unmistakable flutter of movement in my belly. For the first time, I could feel one or both of our babies moving! If that wasn't a sign of good fortune, I didn't know what was.

As the pastor addressed the congregation, Sergei mouthed three words—*I love you*—and my heart sang.

Sergei had always thought that Russians threw the best parties, but after seeing Bianca's family in action, he was ready to change that opinion. He had been apprehensive about mixing their families, friends, and copious amounts of alcohol, but damned if didn't seem to be working beautifully. Not quite believing his eyes, he sat with Bianca on his lap and watched as a tipsy Ivan, a surprisingly agile Three-Fingered Arty and a clapping Boychenko tried to keep up with the intricate steps of a line dance.

"All right," Erin said with a laugh. "I've got to save my man from himself."

Bianca giggled as Erin tried to tug Ivan off the dance floor. When he wouldn't be swayed, she whispered something in his ear. Whatever it was, it worked. The next instant, Ivan swept Erin into his arms and tossed her over his shoulder like a prize. The cheering whoops that erupted from that move filled the reception hall and drowned out the music. Ivan carried her over to their table, grabbed her small clutch and bent down to give Bianca a noisy kiss on the cheek. He smacked Sergei's back and gave a few words of ribald encouragement before leaving the party with his wife slung over his shoulder like some kind of raiding, pillaging Viking.

"If you ever do that to me," Bianca playfully warned with a wagging finger.

Sergei nibbled her fingertip and sucked it gently. "I'll make sure it isn't in public." He settled his hands on her hips. "In fact, I might carry you into our hotel suite like that."

Her eyes flashed with lust. "Well, maybe just once."

He laughed and kissed her hard. When they broke apart, he scanned the big room to make sure everyone was having a good time. Dimitri and Benny had already taken little Sofia home, but Sergei had gotten a chance to hold her. She was the sweetest thing, with her dark hair and blue eyes. He had managed to rock her to sleep while her parents ate an unrushed meal. Sergei had considered it practice for the many sleepless nights he was sure awaited him.

Yuri and Lena were still on the dance floor. He had never seen a couple who enjoyed dancing so much. Remembering Nikolai and Vivian's wedding reception, he fully expected the billionaire to get totally drunk and dance on tables again. He only hoped he was still here when it happened.

In a far corner of the reception hall, he spotted Ten getting cozy with one of Bianca's second or third cousins. She was an older woman who clearly knew the score, so he didn't worry too much. Knowing Ten's reputation, she wouldn't be the only woman he took home tonight.

He had been worried that there wouldn't be much of a showing from his side of the guest list, but his concern had been unfounded. He suspected most of that was due to Nikolai and Vivian. Wherever the king and queen went, so did the court. Tonight, they had a table nearby. Nikolai had his arm around his wife's small waist. His hand rested atop her belly, idly stroking her and soothing the child she carried.

His mother had naturally gravitated that way. She chatted with some of the older wives of the boss's soldiers and captains. Every now and then, she would glance at him and smile. Whatever her earlier reservations about accepting Bianca into the family, she had welcomed her today with open arms and a loving heart.

"That's interesting." Bianca gestured with a tip of her head toward the dance floor. "Look who Vova is dancing with, Sergei."

He smiled at the way she had already taken to calling his brother by his nickname. When he found his brother slow dancing with Zoya, he wasn't that surprised. Vladimir had always been fond of blondes, especially the petite ones like the jewelry designer.

When the song ended, Boychenko approached the table and asked Bianca if she wanted to dance. Sergei patted her hip and encouraged her to enjoy herself. She had hardly left his sight before the boss settled into the empty chair next to him. Nikolai had been nursing the same beer all night. While everyone else got drunk, the boss was always careful, especially with his wife nearby and relying on him to keep her safe.

"It was a beautiful wedding, Sergei." Nikolai leaned back in his chair and stretched his legs. "Perfect."

"Yes." He watched Bianca smiling and laughing with Boy. "The kid can dance."

Nikolai laughed. "He's a good kid. There's potential there."

Once the same had been said about him. Did the boss regret letting him go?

"This isn't the place or the time, Sergei, but Kostya mentioned you had asked him about *nochniye volki*. Is there something I should know?"

He glanced at Nikolai. The older man was asking casually, but his eyes were serious. "This isn't the time," Sergei agreed, "but..." Shifting his position, he faced the boss and explained the issue at hand. "Bianca and her mother are going to meet with Adam Blake at the prison."

Nikolai blinked. "Why?"

"He wants to apologize."

The boss narrowed his eyes. "What a steaming pile of bullshit that is."

"I agree."

"So tell her she isn't going."

"It's not that easy."

"It is," Nikolai replied firmly. "She is your wife. You tell her it's not safe, and she isn't going."

He started to ask the boss how well that worked with Vivian, but bit his tongue instead. "We've discussed it. She's going."

Nikolai glanced away and grunted with disapproval. After a few tense seconds, he turned back and said, "I'll do what I can. The prison he is at doesn't have any of our men in it. I would have to call in favors."

Sergei understood the implicit warning there. If the boss had to call in favors, he was going to come back to Sergei at some point to ask him to repay them. "I understand."

Nikolai nodded. He motioned toward the dance floor. "I think your bride is getting tired." He rose from his seat and patted Sergei's back. "I'll make sure the limo is ready."

Half an hour later, after tossing the bouquet and garter, Sergei rushed Bianca out of the reception hall and into the waiting car. Flower petals and rice pelted them as they made their mad dash away from their party. Like a couple of teenagers, they made out in the backseat and whispered hotly to one another. He couldn't wait to get her up to their suite and strip her out of that beautiful dress. He intended to spend the night reminding her why she had chosen him as her husband.

As promised, he carried her into their suite but he didn't throw her over his shoulder in the end. He feared it wasn't safe in her pregnant state so he cradled her in his arms and gently placed her on the bed. Taking his time, he stripped away her gown and underclothes. He did it reverently and as if unwrapping a special gift.

After all the beer and vodka he'd had, Sergei had to duck into the restroom before things got too interesting. He took off his tux and brushed his teeth while he was in there. With her sensitive stomach, the last thing Bianca wanted was the sour bite of beer in her face.

Rock-hard and aching for her, he stepped out of the bathroom—and discovered Bianca curled on her side and fast asleep. Although disappointed that there would be no wild sex on their wedding night, he didn't mind very much. Her poor body was working overtime to make healthy babies, and it had been a very long day for her.

Shaking his head but smiling, he made sure the door was locked and turned down all of the lights except the one in the bathroom. She might get up in the middle of the night, and he wanted her to be able to see where she was going. He crawled into bed with her and molded his body to hers. She made a soft, kittenish sound of contentment and wiggled back against him.

Kissing her cheek, he draped his arm over her waist and stroked her breast. "Good night, Bianca Sakharovna."

11 CHAPTER ELEVEN

Awash with anxiety, I nervously rubbed my baby bump and glanced at my watch.

"Has he landed yet?" Mama didn't pause the practiced movements of her knitting needles. The clickety-clack of the bamboo sticks smacking together as she worked the long strand of fluffy yarn into a brightly colored baby hat filled the prison waiting room.

"He's supposed to land around five. He's probably just about to take off."

She smiled knowingly. "Five days of separation is about to drive you crazy, isn't it?"

SERGEI II

For most of the week, Sergei had been in Las Vegas with Ivan at a mixed-martial arts championship tournament. Two of Ivan's three fighters had won their divisions. The other had come in second which was still pretty good. I hadn't been able to stomach watching the fights on cable. They reminded me too much of the violent, brutal underground matches I had watched Sergei win. Those were memories I didn't want to relive.

"I can't help it, Mama. I don't like being alone in the house without him." I shifted on the cold hard seat and winced when one of the babies kicked my ribcage. In the six weeks since I had felt that first movement during our wedding, these two babies had gone wild in my belly. Sergei loved to curl up next to me in bed and chase their movements around my stomach with his big hand.

At first, I had felt sort of like a science experiment, but it was the only way he could feel close to them while they were growing inside me. Besides, the look of absolute wonder on his face when the babies kicked back against his fingers made my heart swell with such love. I couldn't wait for the day when he could hold them in his arms and love on them all he wanted.

"Don't you have a security system?"

Actually, I had a security system and round-the-clock guards courtesy of Nikolai. He had two of his men sitting on my house at night and outside the shop during the day. Apparently Erin had been given the same treatment while Ivan was out of town. She wasn't very fond of the men assigned to her, but I rather liked Boy and Danny. Boy had even cut the grass for me one afternoon.

"That's not what I meant, Mama."

She smiled at me again. "I know." She glanced at the pattern sticking out of her purse. "I thought you two were going to do that video message thing on your phones."

"We did." I kept my gaze fixed on my belly and prayed she wouldn't see the flush on my cheeks as I remembered some of the ways we had used technology for our benefit. Before Sergei, I never could have imagined myself stripping down and holding up my phone's camera while I brought myself to climax again and again, but that wicked husband of mine could be awfully persuasive. He used those puppy dog eyes and started telling me how much he missed me. The next thing I knew I was naked on our bed with my fingers—

"Mrs. Bradshaw? Mrs. Sakharov?" Jane Crenshaw, the social worker who had facilitated our meeting with Adam Blake, called our names from behind a fortified glass window. "We're ready for you now."

SERGEI II

As if she visited prisons every day, Mama calmly put away her knitting and rose from her chair. I walked at her side to the locked doors that were buzzed open for us. A male guard took our phones and purses while a female patted us down. They used one of those security wands to check us for hidden weapons. I thought asking Mama to sit down and remove her prosthesis was overkill, but I bit my tongue. Who knew what kind of crazy things people tried to smuggle in here or where they tried to stick them.

Side by side, we trailed Jane into a small room where she went over the procedure and the expectations of the visit again. We had discussed this many times during the preceding weeks via phone conversations and a meeting before one of our support group get-togethers.

Although I wasn't as gung-ho about this meeting as Mama was, I hoped to get something useful out of it. I hadn't seen Adam Blake since the sentencing phase of his trial. We were both older now. I could list all the ways I had changed since then, but I wondered about him. Was he still as angry? Was he still so cruel? Was he a different man now?

We were led in to a secured room where I was going to get my answers. My stomach quivered with nervousness while we sat in our chairs and waited for him to appear. For all of Sergei's assurances, I still feared that Adam had ulterior motives. More than anything, I was terrified that he would bring up his missing brother. What the hell was I supposed to say to that? We had been warned the session today would be taped. What if he tried to get me to incriminate myself in some way?

This was a bad idea. You should have listened to Sergei. He was right. This is madness.

But it was too late to change my mind. The heavy door across the room squeaked and squealed as it was tugged open by a heavyset prison guard. A male nurse pushed a wheelchair into the room. My eyes widened with shock at the frail prisoner sitting in the chair. There was nothing left in this sad shell of the mean, violent young man who had beaten me with his fists and tried to strangle me in that convenience store stockroom.

Gaunt and pale, he looked like he might actually be on the verge of dying. He had been attacked earlier in the year in a prison yard fight. A shiv embedded in his back had left him permanently paralyzed from the waist down and reliant on a colostomy bag. There were ugly, pink scars on his face and neck from recently healed stab wounds. Somehow seeing his pain in the flesh diminished the fleeting joy of retribution I had experienced when I had first heard of the attack on his life.

Did he know that it was his own brother who had ordered it? Did he know that he was nothing more than a pawn in his older brother's stupid power play?

Folding my arms on the table, I held Adam's gaze as he was rolled up to the opposite side. He rested his cuffed hands on the wood and stared back at me. Finally, he spoke. "Bianca." His gaze moved to my mother's face. "Mrs. Bradshaw."

Neither of us said a word. We waited to see what would come of out of his mouth before we extended any promises of forgiveness or grace his way.

With a soft sigh, he weakly began an obviously practiced speech. "I wanted you both to know that there isn't a day that goes by where I don't regret what I did. There isn't a morning that I wake up where I don't think about your son, Mrs. Bradshaw." He swallowed hard, his Adam's apple bobbing up and down in his throat. "I wake up sometimes in the middle of the night, and I remember the way you screamed when I hit you, Bianca. I remember the way you fought so hard to live." He blinked rapidly. "I remember the way your brother jumped in front of you to save you from that bullet."

My heart raced as I listened to my brother's murderer recount the awful things he had done. I didn't know what to say so I pressed my lips together and waited.

"I don't know why I was so angry. I don't know why I thought that people like you deserved to be hurt and bullied and killed." He brought both cuffed hands up to his face and wiped them down his cheeks. "It's stupid. All that rage and pain? It was all so pointless."

Adam interlaced his fingers and placed his hands on the table again. "I know it doesn't change anything. It doesn't bring Perry back. It won't erase the memories of the way I beat you either—but I am sorry. Genuinely," he added soberly. "I am so sorry for what I did."

As I stared at the broken shell of a man in front of me, I felt the anger and hatred I had harbored toward him begin to fade. It wasn't going to happen instantly, but in time, I would feel nothing toward this man. He wasn't worth the effort. It struck me suddenly that his entire existence as a human being had been wasted. The twins kicking and stretching inside me were a re-minder of everything wonderful that I had known in my life, but Adam Blake? He had nothing. He would die alone and empty inside a prison. No one would remember him. His entire history died with him.

I hadn't expected to feel sadness, but there it was. The faint pulse in my chest surprised me, but I em-braced it. He was a human being, the same as me, and it was desperately sad what his life had become.

Silent and stoic, Mama reached across the table and placed a gentle, mothering hand atop his. Adam didn't recoil at the touch. No, he leaned into it and began to weep pathetically. His frail body shook and trembled as he sobbed raggedly.

Mama left her hand atop his. "It's all right," she whispered. "It's all in God's hands now."

Marveling at the strength and goodness my mother displayed and praying that I would someday be as strong as she was, I sat quietly while Adam cried out his remorse. The rest of the visit passed in near silence. Other than his sniffling and a tearfully murmured thank-you, there were no other words spoken between the three of us. Mama and I watched the nurse wheel him out of the room. The guard who had come with him locked the door and left us with the social worker.

"How are you two feeling?" Jane asked gently.

"Lighter," I said honestly. *Relieved that he didn't mention his brother...*

Mama rubbed her finger back and forth across the table. "Finished."

Jane started to talk about closure and the emotions we could expect to process over the next few days, but a shockingly loud alarm interrupted her. Mama and I both jumped in our seats. Pressing a hand to my chest, I glanced around wildly. "What is that?"

"Not good," Jane said honestly. "We should get you two out of here."

Suddenly, Sergei's voice was in my head. He had tried to tell me that prisons were dangerous places. He had tried to make me see that I would be vulnerable inside these walls. Had I listened? No.

With a hand on my belly, I hurried alongside Mama as we were led back down the corridor to the guard room. We could heard snippets of radio traffic and see guards running in the images on the monitors mounted on the far wall. By the looks of it, a small scale riot had erupted in the mid-sized prison. Our belongings were thrust into our hands, and we were hastily pushed into the lobby.

The guard who had been tasked with escorting us tried to put our minds at ease. "You're perfectly safe out here. All of the trouble is contained within the main walls of the prison."

Then why are you walking us to our car?

Out in the parking lot, I noticed that the SUV that had escorted us to the prison was missing. Mama hadn't been happy about the pair following us, but Sergei had explained during Sunday dinner that he had one and only one condition for my going with her. He wanted me watched, just in case. Mama had relented eventually.

I glanced around and frowned. Where had Boy and Danny gone? They had promised to wait for us.

As if reading my mind, the guard asked, "Did you have friends waiting for you?"

"Yes."

"We clear out the parking lots as part of standard riot procedure. I'm sure some of my coworkers asked them to wait outside the gates." The guard checked the backseat of my car and asked me to pop the trunk before sliding down to look under vehicle. I didn't think anyone was crazy enough to try to hitch a ride out under a car but...

"Okay. You ladies are good to go."

"Hon, you be careful going back into there," Mama urged. "Thank you for walking us back to our car."

The guard grinned and moved closer to me. "Oh, I'm not going back in there."

"Are you off shift?" Mama asked.

"No." The guard's grin melted, and his eyes flashed with danger. That was all the warning I had before the guard stepped behind me in one swift move.

I gasped as I felt the hard bite of a gun muzzle against my belly. Back ramrod straight, I held perfectly still while he stuffed his hand into my purse and retrieved the keys. He unlocked my door and wrenched it open.

"What are you doing?"

"Get into the driver's seat right now." He shoved the gun into my side with enough force that I cried out in pain. I felt one of the babies kick at the intrusion. Tears burned my eyes. *Oh, God. No. No. No.*

"Don't even think about it!" The guard warned my mother with a snarl as she opened her mouth to scream. "You get into the rear passenger seat. Not a fucking word out of you or else I'll end this pregnancy about twenty weeks too early."

Mama and I exchanged horrified glances, but did exactly as instructed. The guard slid into the front passenger seat and held the gun on me while he fastened his seatbelt. He leaned over and shoved the keys in the ignition. "You try anything stupid, and I'll blow a hole in your belly. Understand?"

"Yes." With shaking hands, I reached for the shifter and met my mother's fearful gaze in the rearview mirror. "Where are we going?"

"You're going to ease out of this parking lot and go by the guard shack. You stop, but don't even try to ask for help. They've all been paid the same as me." He pressed the gun against my stomach again. "Go."

I didn't dare dawdle. I put the car in drive and moved through the parking lot as if nothing out of the ordinary was happening. Sure enough, the guard at the gate didn't even bat an eye. He pressed the red button and let the car roll right through and off the prison property.

"Now what?"

"Left," he said. "Stay on the highway."

Gripping the steering wheel tightly, I made the turn and gained speed. Not a mile from the prison on the lightly traveled road, I spotted the black SUV Boy and Danny had been driving. It had been run off the road and was flipped upside down. I didn't see either man but there was blood smeared on the windshield. Could they have survived an attack like that?

"Don't worry. They're alive. You'll see them soon."

Confused and frightened, I demanded, "Why are you doing this?"

"Money," the guard said plainly. "Why else?"

"Who do you work for?" If I was going to be killed, I wanted to know who was really pulling the trigger.

"Who do you think?"

"The Night Wolves?"

The guard laughed. "You can't possibly be *that* stupid. They're gone. Done. Finished. Your husband and his friends saw to that after Derek tried to rape and kill you in your store."

Mama's sharp intake of breath surprised the guard. He twisted in his seat and laughed at her. "What? She didn't tell you that Derek Blake and his goons broke into her store and planned to fuck her bloody on top of all those pretty white dresses?"

"You're disgusting," I spat at him. "You leave my mother alone!"

"Or what?" The gun was back against my belly. "Huh? You're not exactly in a prime negotiating position here, sweetheart."

I gritted my teeth and kept driving. He stretched out his legs and waved the gun around as he spoke. "You backed the wrong horse, sugar. You should have found yourself a nice rich cartel husband instead of that giant Russian fucker you chose."

The cartel? What in the world did the cartel want with me? I was nothing. I was nobody. Sergei wasn't even in that life anymore. There was no leverage to be gained from kidnapping me or Mama.

My mind raced as I tried to remember every snippet of news I had read over the last few months. There had been that shooting that had nearly killed strip club owner Besian Beciraj. Sergei had explained that Besian was actually the boss of the local Albanian outfit and also one very wealthy loan shark. He hadn't gone into the details behind that shooting other than to say it had been a cartel assassin gone rogue.

Hadn't there been a link to Hadley Rivera? I had met the insanely rich graphic novelist once or twice at artsy gatherings with Vivian. They ran in similar circles around Houston. Hadley had been at the wrong place at the wrong time when that same assassin had taken shots at her and Finn Connolly.

A few weeks ago, there had been that awful mess on the news about all those cartel-associated gangsters who were killed on the same night. There had been nearly twenty deaths across Houston and dozens more south of the border. The papers had called it an internal coup. When I had asked Sergei about it, he had simply shaken his head and admitted that he had known nothing. He had wanted it to stay that way, too.

Now Nikolai's kind offer to have someone keep an eye on his friends' wives didn't seem so simple. Had he known there was a threat against me? A sickening thought twisted my gut. Was Erin okay? Had they tried to grab her, too? What about Vivian and the baby she carried?

"You ever been to Cabo? I'm thinking that's where I'm going after I make this delivery. I'm going to take my money and run, you know?"

I gawked at the guard. "Are you insane? Are you really trying to make small talk with me while you have a gun pointed at my babies?"

He pointed the gun toward the dash. "There? Happy?"

Before I could answer, Mama shocked me by slamming the sharp tip of her thickest knitting needle into the guard's throat. She screamed like a woman possessed as she embedded her makeshift weapon into his neck. The gun fired, the sound so deafening in the enclosed space that I feared I would never be able to hear again. While the guard choked and slapped at his neck, he waved around the gun. I grabbed his wrist while stomping on the brakes and shoved the gun toward his window. He fired again, blasting out the glass.

Ears ringing and head throbbing, I tried to keep the car under control while watching for that gun, but it was too hard. We spun out of control and veered off the road. We hit a tree so hard that Mama was knocked unconscious when her head whacked the window. My seatbelt and the exploding airbag saved me and the babies. The impact caused the gun to fly out of the guard's hand and out the window.

Panting for air and coughing on the caustic dust now so heavy in the air, I unbuckled my seatbelt with trembling hands. I couldn't hear a damned thing because of the gun shots, and my stomach was so queasy. I managed to get my door open and spilled out of the car and onto the grass. Holding onto the door, I dragged myself into a standing position. My shoes had been knocked off and were jammed up under the pedals, but I didn't even care.

I walked around to Mama's door, using the car for support, but I couldn't get it open. Adrenaline left me shaking and sick. Somehow, I worked up the courage to reach through the shattered window to touch the guard's neck. I felt for a pulse but there was none. He was dead, killed by a knitting needle of all things.

Desperate for help, I walked back around to the driver's side and tried to reach my phone. It had fallen between the guard's feet. Dizzy and sick to my stomach, I weakly stretched out my arm. My belly kept getting in the way, and I put a terrified hand to my bump when I realized I hadn't felt the babies move since the wreck.

"Oh, God. Please." I ran my hands over my belly and pressed down to see if I could elicit a response. Finally, blessedly, I felt one kick and then another. Both babies started to wiggle, and I breathed a sigh of relief.

But my joy was short-lived.

Two SUVs and an oversized floral delivery van barreled toward me. My heart sank when I realized this wasn't a friendly rescue. No, this was my nightmare come true.

I stumbled away from the car and thought about running, but how far would I get? Even when I wasn't pregnant, I could hardly make it two blocks without huffing and puffing. With twins inside me and bare feet? I wasn't going to make it to the first tree before these goons caught up with me.

Placing both hands on my belly in a protective gesture, I gulped and waited. If I could stay alive, Sergei would find me. He would move heaven and earth to bring me and the babies home. Men poured out of the vehicles. I thought of my mother. She was still alive, but these men didn't know that.

One of them approached me cautiously. He had his weapon pointed toward the ground and seemed to pose no immediate risk to me. Deciding that I had to at least try to save my mother, I sobbed, "They're both dead."

He glanced at the mangled car and the bloody mess in the front seat and didn't investigate further. "Come here."

I forced my feet to move. When I was close enough, he grabbed my arm and dragged me toward the delivery van. The doors were jerked open, and I was roughly hauled up and handed over to a pair of heavily armed men standing guard over a small collection of prisoners. The bloody, bound, and unconscious men on the ground looked familiar enough even with the hoods covering their faces. Boy and Danny didn't move, and I prayed they were all right.

My gaze moved to the bench seat on the left side of the cargo space. With her wrists squeezed by zipties, Erin stared up at me with such fear on her beautiful but bruised face. Whoever had given her that black eye and fat lip was a dead man. When Ivan found her—and I knew our men would find us—he was going to unleash that beast he had corralled away when he left the mob.

Shoved down next to Erin, I didn't protest when they bound my hands together or hooked my ankle to a bar with a pair of handcuffs. They weren't going to get any more tears out of me. I was alive. My babies were safe.

And Sergei was going to find us.

Erin reached for my hand. It was awkward with our bound wrists, but we gripped each other's fingers and held tight. We shared a look that communicated what we were both thinking.

These men were going to pay.

12 CHAPTER TWELVE

"Did we leave a bag in the locker room at the arena?" Ivan searched through all the gear they had unloaded.

Pausing his inventory check, Sergei glanced around the stacks of bags and crates in the gear and locker room at the warehouse. He counted them up and nodded. "We're one short."

"I'll have to contact the organizers and see if they can ship it to us." Ivan fished his phone from his pocket and checked it for the hundredth time.

Sergei smiled because he had been doing the same thing. "She still hasn't returned your call?"

"No." Ivan dialed again and held his phone up to his ear. "That's not like her."

Sergei's thoughts turned to Bianca and her mother. He hadn't wanted to pester her too much, especially after her meeting with Adam Blake. He still didn't like it, but he had promised to give his support. He had called once to let her know he was back in Houston. When she was free, he trusted she would call.

Heavy, running footsteps echoed in the empty gym. After hours, there shouldn't have been anyone else in the building. He glanced at Ivan who frowned. Both men turned toward the door in time to see Ten burst into the locker room. Ivan's phone hit the ground with a thud as the sight of Ten's bloodied, bruised body registered. Sergei couldn't believe the man was still walking. He had a fucking gunshot wound in his shoulder and what looked to be a laceration from a knife arcing across his chest. The blood spray on his jeans wasn't his own.

"What the fuck happened to you?" Ivan grabbed a towel and rushed to Ten's side. "You need a hospital."

"Later," Ten growled. "They ambushed us at Vivian's studio."

Sergei's stomach dropped to his knees. "Is she all right? The baby?"

"Fine. They're both fine. I got her to the boss. She's in a safe place." Ten shook his head and put a bloodied hand on Ivan's shoulder. "Arty is in the hospital. Two of his crew members are dead."

Ten glanced at him, and an invisible fist knotted Sergei's stomach. "Boy and Danny are missing. Their SUV was found on the road near the prison. Bianca's car was crashed into a tree. There was a dead prison guard in the front seat. Your mother-in-law was in the back—alive."

Sergei's heart pounded in his chest. "And my wife?"

Ten shook his head. "She's gone. Taken." He looked at Ivan. "With Erin."

No sooner had the words been spoken than Ivan erupted in a fit of rage unlike any Sergei had ever seen. He hefted up an entire bench and swung it at the row of lockers. Sergei flinched when Ivan picked it up again and tossed it against the lockers for a second time. The metal crunched loudly, and the bench clattered as it bounced on the concrete floor. He grabbed one of the locker doors and ripped it off the hinges.

Fearful for his friend, Sergei grabbed Ivan by the shoulders and jerked him around. "Stop! Enough!"

Ivan reared back, and Sergei stiffened for a punch that never came. His friend got control of himself before he crossed that line. Breathing hard, Ivan clenched his fists at his sides. "I swore I would protect her. I promised her no one would ever hurt her again."

"So did I." Sergei pushed down the guilt that threatened to take him out at the knees. Even after he had tried to do everything right, he had still failed Bianca. Like Ivan, he had walked away from that life and reformed himself—but it wasn't enough. It was never going to be enough.

Ivan snarled at Ten. "Where the fuck is Kolya?"

"He's waiting for us." Ten's black eyes practically gleamed with murderous intent. "It all ends tonight."

A cold ball settled in the pit of Sergei's stomach. This wasn't a war the boss had started, but it was one that he was going to finish. This was a mess that Maksim Prokhorov and Romero Valero had tipped off with their power plays and intrigues. Sergei had purposely ignored the rumors he heard around the gym and on the construction sites. He hadn't wanted to know what those two old fucks were up to down south, but now? Now he was furious. The consequences of their games had spilled onto the streets of Houston.

Tonight those streets would run red with blood. Innocent or guilty, it wouldn't matter. As Sergei slid behind the wheel of Ten's SUV, he felt the enforcer's blood soaking into his jeans. It wasn't the first time he had had another man's blood on his skin. It wouldn't be the last.

To save Bianca and their babies, there was no line he wouldn't cross tonight.

Shaking with cold, I ignored the throbbing in my hands and my dry mouth. My bladder screamed to be emptied. Every movement the babies made was sheer agony at this point, but I was glad to feel the reassuring kicks and stretches. I glanced around the refrigerated room where they were holding us. Erin's teeth chattered together, and she squirmed incessantly to try to stay warm.

We had been pushed into this freezing cold room after arriving at the abandoned dairy plant. The scent of sour milk hung ripe in the air. I wasn't sure what was being hidden away in those vats now, but knowing the cartel? I guessed drugs or guns. Maybe both.

On the far end of the space, Boy and Danny sagged against their bonds. They had been strung up by their wrists and hung from meat hooks. I prayed that gagging and blindfolding them was the worst they would do to the men. I didn't think I could hold it together if those cartel guys started to beat or torture them.

"What do you mean he's not coming?"

Erin and I glanced at each other as a man's booming voice filtered through the open door of the refrigerated room. We listened carefully as the men who had taken us captive argued outside.

"This is bullshit. He ran? Ran where?"

"I don't know, man. The word is coming down the chain that *El Jefe* disappeared this morning. He went underground. He's gone."

"And no one thought to fucking tell us *before* we crossed the Russians?" The man who seemed to be in charge sounded panicked. "What if he didn't run? What if they got to him? I never trusted Salas or Contreras. Lalo and Hector were the only two who survived those attacks last month. I still fucking think they shot each other to make it look like they had been attacked too."

"Who cares? Either way, man, we're fucked. The guys we sent after the boss's old lady never made it back. We lost the guard which means the rest of the guys we paid off at the prison are going to squeal. Our men outside? How long do you think they stick around once they find out Lorenzo didn't send reinforcements?"

"What do we do? Cut them loose?"

Erin and I exchanged hopeful looks.

"Fuck that! They've seen our faces. We slit their throats and go."

Oh, no. Please. Please not that. My bound hands rested on the curve of my stomach. Frantic, I looked around the room for something, anything, to help us out of this.

"Man, I got no problem killing the two soldiers, but the girls? One of them is pregnant. I don't kill babies."

"Do you know who Ivan Markovic is? Do you know what he'll do to you if he finds out you punched his wife? He'll rip your balls off and shove them down your throat. And the other one? I saw her husband fight once. He cracked a man's sternum with one punch. One. Punch." The man chortled loudly. "No, I'm not sticking around for that show. We kill them, and we go."

Erin and I tensed as the two men came into the room. The light-skinned blond already had his knife out. The other one, the man who had approached me on the side of the road, glanced uneasily around the room. His distaste for killing us was clear enough.

"Look, Chris, maybe we should think about this," he pleaded. "They're worth more alive than dead." He looked at Boy and Danny who had gone still when the men had entered the room. "The girls, at least."

"What? You want to ransom them back, Juan?" Despite the derision in his voice, Chris lowered his knife. "You think they would pay?"

"Ivan Markovic is rich, right? And the other one? Sergei? He's in tight with Kalasnikov. That's lots of deep pockets we can rob."

Chris seemed to consider it. "What if they won't pay?"

"Then we sell them," Juan replied with a shrug. "The skinny one is really pretty. I bet Tran would pay good money for some young pussy like that. She's...what, twenty-three? Twenty-four? Not as good as the teenagers he likes to pick up on spring break, but she's fresh and clean."

"And that one?" Chris pointed the knife at me. "I doubt the market for pregnant whores is very high."

"No," Juan agreed, "but I bet we could make nice money off those babies. I heard people pay tens of thousands of dollars for newborns. She's got two of them inside her. You could have one and I could take the other."

Listening to them talk about my babies like they were puppies to be sold to the highest bidder made me sick. Next to me, Erin shuddered with disgust. How in the world did men get this cruel? How did they become so devoid of feeling that they could discuss trafficking one of us and selling babies on the black market as easily as if they were talking about a football game?

"Keeping her alive is the easy part," Chris said as he knelt down in front of me. The knife came dangerously close to my belly, and I whimpered. He seemed to enjoy my fear and pressed the sharp edge against my shirt. "What happens when the babies are ready to come?"

"We could have them taken out. It can't be that hard to find a doctor to do it for us. When it's done, we let her bleed out."

Chris glanced back at his cohort. "Seems like a waste. She might be able to make more money on her back." Standing up, Chris grabbed my arms and hauled me to my feet. "Get the skinny one. Let's go."

Juan snatched up Erin and dragged her into a standing position. He gestured to Danny and Boy. "What about those two?"

"We'll send the others back here to watch them. We tell the guys we're taking these two to a new drop-off spot. Let them be the ones to greet the Russians." Chris roughly shoved me forward. "Because you and I both know that cleaner they keep on their payroll will find this place sooner or later."

Kostya. I didn't know the silent, brooding man very well, but Vivian seemed to think he was the most dangerous soldier among Nikolai's men. Could he find us so quickly?

"Go!" Chris kicked my backside, and I stumbled forward. "I'm not carrying your fat ass."

Glaring back at him, I silently called him every curse word I could think of in that moment. Dizzy and cold, I made my feet move toward the doorway. I passed through the thick, wide plastic strips that hung there—and was promptly grabbed by two brawny and very familiar arms.

Sergei!

Before I could even process what had happened, I was passed into different arms and pushed up against a concrete wall. The hallway outside the refrigerated room was dimly lit. Dazed, I blinked rapidly and finally realized it was Nikolai who now shielded my body with his own. I glanced toward the door I had just exited and watched as Chris walked out, completely unaware of the retribution that awaited him.

Sergei snatched him by the front of the shirt and lifted the heavy-set man as if he were a sack of potatoes. He slammed Chris against the wall across from me before punching him in the ribs. The man cried out in agony as his bones were cracked and crunched like an empty soda can. Still, Sergei didn't stop.

He pummeled the man who had threatened to steal and sell our babies on the black market. When Chris slumped against the wall, Sergei threw him onto the floor and leapt atop him like a jungle cat tearing into prey. He pounded the man's face. A furious roar unlike any I had ever heard erupted from Sergei's throat. Chris coughed and gurgled, but still Sergei showed no mercy. He was going to kill him. He was going to beat this man to death right in front of me.

Pushing away Nikolai's hands, I shoved out of his protective embrace and slowly crossed to my husband's side. He flung his fist back, and I wrapped my arms around his thick arm. He jerked hard and nearly took me down to the ground. At the last moment, he realized it was me. I wound my arm around his neck and hauled him into a kneeling position.

Pressing my cheek to his blood-spattered one, I hugged him from behind. "Enough, Sergei. It's over. He's had enough."

Overcome with emotion, Sergei spun around and embraced me. He drove me back against the wall, his hands cradling my back and cushioning the sudden impact. He rubbed his face against my belly, nuzzling against me like a dog would its master. When he gazed up at me finally, there were tears in his dark eyes. Fear, relief, guilt, love—I could see his warring emotions playing out on his handsome face.

Even though all hell was breaking loose around us, we only had eyes for each other. He placed his battered, bloodied hands on my belly and tenderly kissed it. I ran my fingers through his hair and let the tears come. I didn't know what was going to happen now, but I trusted that with Sergei at my side, it would be all right in the end.

13 CHAPTER THIRTEEN

Four Months Later

"How many hooded towels do we need?" Sergei asked as he sorted through another pile of baby shower gifts. It had taken him half an hour to bring in all the bags and boxes from the party they had attended that afternoon at Samovar. Now Bianca sat on the couch in the living room with her swollen feet propped on an ottoman and helped him sort through everything.

"We're having twins, Sergei. We need twice as much of everything."

"But where are we supposed to put it all?" He made a stack of blue towels and pink towels on the coffee table. "Between your mother and mine, the nursery is overflowing. If this keeps up, I'm going to have to convert one of the guest rooms to a walk-in closet for our babies."

"I've heard worse ideas. You could do built-in shelves on three walls, but you would have to change the flooring. Oh, and maybe add a new window?"

Glancing over at her, he was glad to see that she had a teasing smile on her face. With all the nesting she had been doing lately, he couldn't always tell. Last week, she had asked him to move every single piece of furniture in the house, upstairs and downstairs, so she could vacuum and sweep behind and under them. He had tried to tell her that their babies wouldn't even notice the dust, but she had turned on the waterworks and that was that.

Bianca yawned loudly. "I'm beat."

Sergei studied the mess in their living room and made an executive decision. "This will be here in the morning. Let's go upstairs."

She perked up at that. "Will you rub my back?"

Rub my back had become her code word for sex. No matter how innocently it started, every back rub seemed to lead to lovemaking. Not that he was complaining. He had heard that some women preferred to

shut down bedroom activities as their pregnancies pro-
gressed, but Bianca was the complete opposite. There
were nights when he was the one pleading exhaustion.
She had become absolutely insatiable.

"Come on." He grabbed her hands and hauled her
into a standing position. The heavy curve of her huge
belly seemed lower to him than it had yesterday, but
he couldn't be sure. It might have been the cut of her
top that fooled his eye.

With his hand against her lower back, he led her
upstairs and into the master bathroom. She happily
stood still while he stripped her naked and got the
shower ready. He helped her inside and then shucked
his clothing to join her. Never one to waste a chance to
get his hands on her, Sergei lathered up his palms and
made sure every last inch of her luscious body was
squeaky clean. He spent a little extra time on his favorite parts.

After that nightmarish night where he thought he
might lose her and the babies, Sergei never took these
moments for granted. Flashes of memories he would
rather forget tormented him. Like him, Ivan had to be
dragged off the man who had manhandled and beaten
Erin. Kostya had done what he did best and cleaned
up the scene, but Bianca and Erin had been forced to
sit and wait in a different location for a police rescue
that was orchestrated by the cleaner. Sergei had joined

Ivan at one of the bars Besian owned to establish air-tight alibis that included getting into a brawl to explain away their bruised hands.

The women had spent the night in a hospital for observation. He had stayed awake the entire time and simply watched Bianca sleep while listening to the reassuring beats of the babies' hearts on the monitors attached to her. When he had gone to visit his mother-in-law on a different floor, she had been sure to let him know how very disappointed she was that he had dragged Bianca into something so terrible. He had taken it like a man. No amount of guilt she heaped onto his shoulders would ever surpass his own. Slowly but surely, he was earning back Mona's trust.

When he and Ivan had discussed that night a few days later, both men had come to the conclusion that there truly was no escape from the dark deeds of their pasts. That sin was stained deep on their souls. They could leave Houston and strike out in places where they knew no one, but even that wasn't foolproof.

The city had quieted down after that night, but Sergei continued looking over his shoulder. Sooner or later, his past would return to haunt him again, but he refused to focus on the what-ifs. He was living in the moment.

And right now, he had a beautiful, naked and very sexy woman panting in his bed.

Grinning wickedly, he slid down between Bianca's thighs to taste her. She made those sweet, whimpering noises as he flicked her clit and probed her pussy with his tongue. She responded so quickly these days. Always primed for his touch, he could bring her off with only a few minutes of sensual torment. It had become something of a game for him to see how fast he could make her scream.

"Sergei." Her thighs tensed under his hands. "Sergei. Oh, baby. Right there. Right—*oh*."

Perfect. He lapped at her cunt while she rocked and screamed with ecstasy. Shuddering and breathing hard, she let him flip her over without protest. He grabbed two pillows and shoved them under her belly and hips to give her some support. She wiggled her big bottom, and he smacked her plump cheeks, making her yelp and giggle.

Pushing her thighs apart, he nudged his cock between them and stroked it against her slick folds. She had grown so sensitive that he had stopped taking her as deeply or hard. He carefully entered her slick heat and groaned at the wonderful sensation. Snug in her cunt, he took his time tonight. Unrushed and unhurried, he set a languid, easy pace that let them both enjoy a slow build toward passion.

When Bianca started to claw at the sheets and twist them in her fists, he slipped a hand between her thighs to help her find that release she craved. His fingertips danced around her clit and settled on a rhythm that made her inner walls clench. Biting his lower lip, he thrust a little faster and changed the angle. She cried out and pushed back against him, urging him to stay right there.

She shouted his name as she came, and he loosened the stranglehold on his own orgasm. He chased her right over the edge, coming with her and pounding into her until they were both falling forward on jelly-like legs. He cocooned her lush body in his arms and enjoyed her soft, feminine warmth.

When she shifted a short time later, he put his hand against her lower back and began to massage the spot that gave her so much trouble. The pregnancy had been relatively easy, all things considered. She had managed to avoid gestational diabetes and blood pressure problems. The babies were measuring ahead, but given his size and that of his brothers at birth, he wasn't all that surprised. Big babies were simply in his genes.

The relief she received from his back rub lulled her to sleep. He slipped away from her just long enough to check the house one final time and turn off the lights. When he got back into bed, he pushed a pillow between her knees and sidled up to her back. He slung his arm over her waist and let his hand rest on her belly.

Sometime later, he heard Bianca calling his name. Bleary-eyed, he reached for her but grabbed the blanket instead. Sitting up, he realized she wasn't in bed. His gaze traveled to the bathroom where the light could be seen under the door.

"Bianca?"

"Sergei, can you bring me some clean clothes?"

Clean clothes? He glanced at the clock. It was one in the morning. Why did she need clothes at this time of night?

Shoving out of bed, he crossed their room and opened the bathroom door. He found her standing in a puddle and rubbing a wet washcloth down her inner thighs. For a moment, he wasn't quite sure what to think. Finally, it hit him. "Is that—?"

"My water broke," she said, shockingly calm. "I think all that back pain was actually early labor."

"What?" He rushed to her side, grabbing a towel from the bar and dropping it onto the puddle there. "Are you sure?"

"I woke up forty minutes ago with cramps. They're getting stronger. I'm just glad I had to use the bathroom. I came in here, felt a pop and then it gushed out everywhere." She wrinkled her nose. "This would have ruined the floors."

"Who cares about the floors? But isn't it too early?"

"Thirty-six weeks is a little early, but we're having twins. That's not so uncommon."

He tried to remember everything from the books and classes, but his mind blanked. With a sweet smile, she touched his face. "Get me some clean clothes, please. We need to shower and pack our bags. I'll call the hospital to let them know we're coming in like the doctor said, okay?"

"Okay." He dumbly nodded his head and headed toward their bedroom to get the clothes she wanted.

"Sergei?"

He stopped in the doorway and glanced back at her. "Yes?"

"Don't panic. We can do this."

"I'm not panicking." He moved into the bedroom and started digging through the closet for something comfortable for her to wear. He picked up the list she had started for her hospital bag. He thought of the mess downstairs. There was so much to do and no time to do it.

Shit. I'm panicking.

Don't panic.

"We can do this," he repeated softly. If Bianca said it, then it had to be true.

Sleepy and sore, I let my eyes adjust to the early morning sunlight now spilling through the window of our post-partum suite. The pain meds were starting to wear off, and soon I would feel the true pangs of recovering from a C-section. Though I had wanted a vaginal birth, the babies had had other ideas. Not long after being admitted to the hospital, my obstetrician had come in to check on me. Thankfully, she had been on call, so I had a familiar face treating me.

By palpating my belly, she had been able to tell the babies weren't in very good positions. An ultrasound had confirmed her diagnosis. Our son had both feet up near his head and his bottom down near my cervix, and our daughter had actually been slanted diagonally with her feet under my ribcage. For the safety of the babies and myself, a C-section had been recommended. The idea of surgery scared me, but I had chosen to err on the side of caution.

Everything after that was something of a blur. Sergei had been whisked away to change while I was taken to an operating room and prepped. Inserting the spinal block had been less than fun, but it hadn't been too bad. As they draped and prepared me for the surgery, I focused on the outcome.

Once Sergei had joined me, the whole thing had happened fairly quickly. Our daughter had been born first and then our son. Both were nearly seven pounds and so very long. Their cries had inspired my own. When Sergei had left to walk them to the nursery, I had been sad, but I reminded myself there was a lifetime to enjoy them.

Now, here I was, reclining in bed and starting to finally feel my legs again. Seated in the chair next to my bed, Sergei cradled our babies in his massive arms. They looked so unbelievably small against those brawny muscles. Both babies had dark, curly hair and skin that seemed to be a shade closer to mine than his. Our son had his bone structure, and I swore our daughter resembled Galina.

Soon our friends and family would descend on our hospital room, but right now, it was just the four of us. *My family.* The thought made me smile and filled me with such contentment.

Sergei finally stopped gazing at our babies and looked up at me. His eyes were glimmering with tears. He wasn't the most emotional man, so seeing him on the verge of crying surprised me. "What's wrong, baby?"

"Nothing," he said gruffly. "Nothing at all."

Very carefully, he stood up and brought the babies to me. He kissed our son before handing him over. I still couldn't believe this perfect, beautiful thing had been created and grown inside me. Cradling our daughter, Sergei bent down and captured my mouth in a lingering, loving kiss. We shared a secret smile and a look that needed no words.

I understood the tears in Sergei's eyes because now I had them too. This was happiness. Our journey together had taken us to some truly wonderful places, but this? This was the absolute best of them. I couldn't wait to see what life had in store for us next.

14 WHAT'S IN A NAME?

Bonus Short Story!

"Sergei, we have to pick names. Today," Bianca added urgently. "The nurses are giving me funny looks, and the twins are going to start thinking their names are Girl and Boy!"

Smiling down at his freshly bathed daughter, Sergei used the gentlest touch possible to carefully slip her arms into the frightfully pink outfit. His fingers trembled slightly as he worked, and he was glad he had his back to Bianca so she wouldn't see how nervous all of this made him. Despite assurances from the nurses and doctors that his daughter was a big baby for a twin, she looked so small. He held his hand up against her body and marveled at the way he dwarfed her minute form.

"What should we call you? Hmm?" He addressed her in the same tender way he often spoke to Bianca. It was a tone of voice he reserved for the ones he loved.

"Well don't even think about suggesting Mouse again," Bianca warned. "Her ears are not that big."

Sergei traced one of her little ears. They were bigger than her brother's and did, in fact, remind him of a sweet little mouse. Bianca, however, didn't find that funny in least.

"She'll grow into them," he decided. "Won't you, *myshka?*"

"Sergei!"

He laughed softly, the sound drawing his baby girl's attention. After nursing and a bath, she hovered on the edge of sleep again. Her dark eyes tried to focus on his face. When she gripped his finger with her tiny hand, he swallowed hard and tried to breathe. With one little touch, she completely owned him.

So lost in her sweet face, he didn't realize she had kicked her legs out of the onesie until one of them whacked his arm. Two days old, and she was already an escape artist who could rival a cuffed and blindfolded Kostya! Shaking his head with amusement, he grasped her small legs and slowly worked them back inside the cozy outfit.

His thick fingers fumbled over the miniscule snaps. "Do all of their clothes have these?"

"Have what, baby?"

"These ridiculous little snaps," he replied, fighting to get them to latch. "My big hands aren't good at this sort of thing."

"Sweetheart, you seem to forget that I'm very well acquainted with all the wonderful things those big hands of yours can do. A couple of tiny snaps shouldn't be a problem for you."

Her saucy reply brought a smile to his face. He glanced back at his wife and grinned as she lovingly stroked their son's head while he nursed. Propped up in the hospital bed, she used one of those oddly shaped pillows to support the baby who greedily drank the nourishing milk from her breast. When she shifted in bed, he caught her slight wince of pain and wondered when it was going to get better for her.

Nothing about their labor or delivery experience had gone the way she had envisioned. Nursing wasn't working as well either, but she was trying so hard. Guilt gnawed at his stomach. His part in this parenthood business had been so easy compared to hers. For him, it had been nothing but pleasure and happiness. Bianca was the one who had gone through months and months of exhausting work carrying their twins. She had endured the pain of labor and now had to recover from surgery neither of them had expected.

Bianca had done it all without complaint—and he was utterly fucking amazed by her. Just when he thought she couldn't possibly make him more proud to be her husband, she proved that she was even stronger and more brilliant than he had ever imagined.

As if sensing his gaze, she glanced up at him. In all the time they had been together, these two days and three nights in the hospital were the longest stretch she had gone without makeup or styling her hair or wearing one of those sexy, classy outfits that sent heat rolling through his belly.

Somehow seeing Bianca with her hair pulled back into a messily brushed ponytail and her face bare only enhanced her beauty. No woman had ever looked as wonderful as she did in that moment. His heart swelled in his chest, thumping against his ribcage, and he wondered what the hell he had done to be this lucky.

They shared a quiet, knowing smile before turning their gazes back to their children. He finally managed to get his daughter dressed. Remembering the way his mother-in-law had taught him, he swaddled her in one of the blush pink receiving blankets Yuri and Lena had given them before carefully, gently, lifting her into his arms. He cradled her protectively and nuzzled the top of her head, brushing his lips against the soft tuft of dark hair crowning her head. He inhaled the sweet scent of his *myshka* before pressing a loving kiss to her cheek.

He settled into the rocking chair next to the bed and enjoyed the fatherly moment. Even after she fell asleep, he continued to rock her. He couldn't stop staring at her beautiful little face. There was so much of Bianca in her, but he could see a little of himself there too.

"What are you thinking about?" Bianca wondered, her voice barely louder than a whisper. She rubbed her thumb along their son's jaw, coaxing him to continue nursing in the hopes it would encourage her milk supply to increase.

"I'm thinking that I never thought I could ever love anyone as much as I love you," he answered honestly. "But now I see I was wrong. It's a different kind of love," he added, "but it's strong."

"Unconditional," she said. "It's unconditional love. It's complete and whole and protective love."

He nodded. "Yes."

"I liked Aleksandr. From your list of names," she explained. "It's a good name for a boy."

Secretly, he was pleased she liked that name. It was the one he had wanted most for his first-born son.

"We'll have to spell it the American way so it's easier for him in school."

"All right." She hesitated. "What about his middle name? Are we going to do it your way?"

He huffed with amusement at the memory of that conversation. A few weeks ago, he had tried to explain the Russian naming conventions and had only succeeded in confusing the hell out of her. "No, I don't think Sergeyevich and Sergeyovna would be very good for middle names. Not in Texas, at least," he added with a grin.

"No," she agreed sadly. "But we should make sure they know what their names would have been like if they had been born in your country."

"They'll know," he assured her. They had already decided the children would be raised bilingual and immersed in both cultures. That wouldn't be difficult to accomplish with Dimitri and Nikolai's children so close in age to the twins. Vivian had jokingly suggested painting Moscow murals on the walls of the playroom she had decorated at the home she shared with the boss for their future playdates.

Hoping Bianca wouldn't cry, he cleared his throat and offered the first name he had been considering for their son. "Bradshaw, Bianca. His first name should be Bradshaw and his middle name can be Alexander."

She lifted her surprised gaze to his face. "Brad-shaw? But—"

"Your father and brother are gone. You're the last Bradshaw. It's right for our son to carry on your family's name."

She bit her plump lower lip to squelch the wobbling that he could easily see. "Thank you, Sergei." Looking down at their son, she murmured his name with an amused smile, "Bradshaw Alexander Sahkarov. That's quite a mouthful."

He snorted with laughter. "Sounds pretentious, yes?"

"No, it's perfect. It's a strong name for the strong man he'll be someday. But—maybe we should give him a nickname? Alex?"

Sergei shook his head. "Sasha."

"Sasha," she happily repeated. "I like that."

"Good. That's done. Now we get to name you, *myshka*." He grazed his fingertips across their daughter's wispy hair. "Your top choice for her was Isabella. My top choice was Irina. Can we compromise? Isabella Irina?"

Bianca grinned. "I like that." Her loving gaze fell on their daughter. "Bella."

"Bella," he agreed and tucked her in a little tighter to his chest.

"Sasha and Bella," Bianca murmured lovingly.

Feeling happier and more content than he ever had in his life, Sergei snuggled his sweet Bella and rocked slowly. His gaze drifted from her cherubic sleeping face to Bianca and Sasha. His wife had closed her dress and cuddled their son while he dozed in a warm, milk-induced coma.

Pride and love overwhelmed him. After all the heartache and loss they had known, these innocent new lives brimming with possibility filled him with such hope for their future.

Our family. Overjoyed, he hugged Bella and kissed her cheek. My family.

And there was no line he wouldn't cross to keep them all safe...

ROXIE RIVERA

AN AUTHOR'S NOTE

Thanks so much for picking up *Sergei II*! I hope you enjoyed the continuation of Sergei and Bianca's tale.

The *Her Russian Protector* series continues with Nikolai II, Kostya and Alexei, coming out in summer and fall 2014.

ABOUT THE AUTHOR

A *New York Times* and *USA Today* bestselling author, I like to write super sexy romances and scorching hot erotica. I live in Texas with a husband who could easily snag a job as an extra on History Channel's new *Viking* series and a sweet but rowdy four-year-old.

I also have another dirty-book writing alter ego, Lolita Lopez, who writes deliciously steamy tales for Ellora's Cave, Forever Yours/Grand Central, Mischief/Harper Collins UK, Siren Publishing and Cleis Press.

You can find me online at www.roxierivera.com.

Roxie's Backlist

Her Russian Protector

Ivan (Her Russian Protector #1)

Dimitri (Her Russian Protector #2)

Yuri (Her Russian Protector #3)

A Very Russian Christmas (Her Russian Protector #3.5)

Nikolai (Her Russian Protector #4)

Sergei (Her Russian Protector #5)

Sergei II

Nikolai, Volume 2 (Her Russian Protector #6)—Coming June 2014

Kostya (Her Russian Protector #7)—Coming Summer 2014

Alexei (Her Russian Protector #8)—Coming Fall 2014

Danila (Her Russian Protector #9)—Coming Fall 2014

The Fighting Connollys

In Kelly's Corner (Fighting Connollys #1)

In Jack's Arms (Fighting Connollys #2)

In Finn's Heart (Fighting Connollys #3

Debt Collection

Collateral (Debt Collection #1)

Collateral II (Debt Collection #2)—Coming Soon

Past Due (Debt Collection #3)—Coming Soon

Seduced By...

Seduced by the Loan Shark

Seduced by the Loan Shark 2—Coming Soon!

Seduced by the Congressman

Seduced by the Congressman 2

Erotica

ROXIE RIVERA